THE 2nd FUGITIVE

A UNIT 22 THRILLER

THE 2nd FUGITIVE

A UNIT 22 THRILLER

MAINAK DHAR

Anecdote
Publishing House
For the love of quality reading!

Anecdote
Publishing House
For the love of quality reading!

Anecdote Publishing House
2nd Floor 2/15 Lane no. 2 Ansari Road, Daryaganj-110002
Email: info@anecdotepublishinghouse.com
Website: anecdotepublishinghouse.com

Published by Anecdote Publishing House

First Edition 2024
ISBN 978-81-973806-4-8
MRP ₹ 350

Book Promoted and Marketed by Champ Readers Pvt. Ltd.
Edited by Amy Brantley
Cover design by Damonza.com
Layout by Graphic Tailor
Printed by Thomson Press (India) Ltd, New Delhi

FSC
www.fsc.org
MIX
Paper | Supporting responsible forestry
FSC® C010615

What made The 1St Assassin a National bestseller?

"Breath-taking tale of espionage and conspiracy... a mixture of high action, deep intrigues, dark humor that will delight thriller lovers...crisp action, thought-provoking plot, and compelling protagonist will leave readers hungry for more."

—Book Life by Publishers Weekly

"Grab a bag of popcorn because you won't stop flipping through the pages...a gripping, action-packed thriller, this is a must-read...the most intriguing plot, with ingenious and mind-blowing twists. There is action, thrills, suspense, and so much more in this magnificent piece of work."

—Readers' Favorite, US

"Dhar packs the plot with relentless action electrifyingly depicted—the book seems written for the big screen."

—Kirkus Reviews

"The author writes with clarity yet pulls you in as a reader. There's a great assassination plot going on, some interesting characters, and plenty of action to keep the pace moving quickly along. Definitely a fun and enticing read that keeps your attention."

—Amazon Vine Voice review

"One of the year's top conspiracy thrillers."

—Best Thriller Book Awards

Contents

Episode One
A Case Of Cathisophobia 1

Episode Two
Beauty & The Baboon 29

Episode Three
The Don 56

Episode Four
Cars, Trains & Planes 84

Episode Five
Georgie Goes To War 112

Episode Six
The Wisdom Of Kautilya 141

Episode Seven
Russian Roulette 171

Episode Eight
Dust To Dust 201

Episode Nine
Form 42 228

Episode Ten
The Spy Who Loved Me 262

Author's Note
The Real-Life Unit 22 279

About Mainak Dhar 283

As Always, for

Puja & Aaditya

"Then out spake brave Horatius,
The Captain of the Gate:
To every man upon this earth
Death cometh soon or late.
And how can man die better
Than facing fearful odds,
For the ashes of his fathers,
And the temples of his gods"

Lays of Ancient Rome by Thomas Babington Macaulay

EPISODE ONE

A CASE OF CATHISOPHOBIA

When my boss told me that I could sit at a desk and not worry about killing people anymore, he didn't realize that I preferred killing people to sitting at a desk.

I had spent almost a decade serving my country. First in the army, following in my father's footsteps and proudly wearing the maroon beret of the Paras. Then I joined the Special Frontier Force, where I found a new home among men who were brothers more than colleagues. We went on missions that never officially existed and killed enemies we never officially killed. They gave me a bunch of medals, but I did what I did not for the medals or for the glory. There was no glory because nobody really knew what we did anyways. I did what I did because my brothers needed me, and I was there for them. A mission went wrong, which left two of my brothers dead on my watch, and though I avenged their deaths, I was left broken inside, their loss driving home to me just how guilty I felt at staying alive when those around me, better men than me, died. I found myself fighting demons in my head far deadlier than any enemy I had met on the battlefield. I was able to claw back to sanity due to my mother, who was my pillar of strength, giving me courage even as she battled cancer and a new mission which helped me rediscover who I was. That mission saw me meet and lose a woman I fell in love with, an American Secret Service Agent called Amy, but brought back into focus that I needed to focus not on myself but on the many people around me whom I could help with the skills I had.

"Sen, you're killing your keyboard again. What has that poor keyboard done to piss you off anyways?"

I stopped typing and looked up at Salil Murthy grinning, standing at the door to my office. Salil was a fellow officer at the Research & Analysis Wing, and he had been left scarred by our previous mission as well. Bomb fragments in his back had left him with a stiff gait and a scar across his face. Fragments from an explosion that had killed my boss, an attack which would have killed me as well had Salil not gone in my place. He had also been stabbed in the thigh while saving my mother. We had been friends ever since I joined this unit, but that act had made him a brother.

"I'm doing this report the boss wanted. This Form 42 or whatever it is."

He sat down across me and looked on as I continued butchering the keyboard. Given the many years I had spent learning martial arts and then serving in the army, I was pretty good with my hands. I mean, I can disassemble and assemble a Glock in the dark, I can break a man's neck in four different ways, and I can make a booby trap out of a bottle of rum, a lighter and a shoelace. However, what I am terrible at is pecking at a keyboard. Especially when I hated filling up long, bureaucratic forms almost as much as I hated sitting at a desk for hours at a stretch.

Salil had poured himself some of the coffee I had brewed, and continued watching, a smile on his face. I looked up at him and scowled.

"So, you will steal my coffee and then sit there and laugh at me?"

He laughed out loud.

"Sen, you've lost it. Just leave half the fields blank, especially the ones which you think only matter to some fat idiot in an office in Delhi. The stuff that matters will get to those who need to act on it anyways."

A lightbulb went off in my head and I finished the form in ten minutes, and Salil was still there, grinning when I pressed the 'send' button to pass the file on to whichever bureaucrat it was destined for.

"Lunch?"

"Done."

Lunch, as often was the case with Salil, happened to

be greasy kababs at Tahir's Kabab Corner in Nizamuddin. It was run down, dirty, surrounded by shady looking shops with shadier looking shopkeepers, but it had the best kababs near the office. Also, the ambience, or lack of it, meant that we didn't run the risk of bumping into anyone from work and could chat freely.

"Sen, what does it feel like being the boss in Sean's place?"

I hadn't really thought about that. For someone like me, getting a bigger cabin or a fancier nameplate hadn't meant much. Srini Iyer, our boss, had asked me to step up and fill some of the roles that my previous boss, Sean D'Silva had played, and I had been happy to help. Sean had been a pain in the neck at times, but nobody deserved to go the way he did, in a bomb explosion six months ago when we had been on the hunt for assassins who had come in to attack the US President. That train of thought took me to Amy and other things I'd rather forget. Salil seemed to read my expression.

"Hey, I'm sorry. I shouldn't have brought it up."

I would have resented almost anyone else bringing up those events. When a Minister had fawned over me and told me I'd get many medals for my role in unmasking the conspiracy behind those killings, I had wanted to kill him with my bare hands. Many good men had died during those days. Correction. Not just good men, but also one special woman- Amy. She had been a Secret Service agent I had fallen in love with, only to discover that she was part of the conspiracy. She had died saving my life, teaching me that people are much more complex than our simplistic notions of good or evil.

"It's okay, Salil. You were there, you are there. You're one of us. I know you understand in a way others won't."

He nodded as I continued, perhaps realizing that I was finally opening up about what was on my mind.

"Amy was a special woman. Shame that she made some of the choices she did, but with all that she went through, who am I to judge her? At the end, she came through for me. My earlier life in uniform was simpler-with easily defined enemies my bosses pointed out for me. Those days when we were hunting the assassins taught me that the world is more complex than that. There are enough people ready to prey on the weak, people who may never fire a gun, but who pull the strings in the background, like that bastard Walker and his masters, whoever they might be. That taught me that I could still serve, still be useful."

Salil took a big bite of his kabab.

"You are an idealist, Sen, but the world needs more people like you. You do realize that whoever actually paid Walker to assassinate the US President may never be revealed? They're too big, too rich, and too connected."

I looked him in the eye, and he averted his gaze at the expression I had more so than the words I said.

"Enough bastards out there to kill to even the score a bit and let them know there are sheepdogs watching over the sheep they take to be easy prey."

"Enough talk about killing, man. How's Aunty doing?"

I smiled. That had been the other thing that had kept me going. My mother had recovered, both due to the treatment she had been on, and perhaps, even more so, due to the fact that I seemed to have found my footing again.

"She's doing great."

"Do you know what your problem is, Sen?"

"I guess you've decided to tell me whether I want your opinion or not, so tell me, oh wise one, what ails me?"

"You suffer from a case of Cathisophobia."

I kept my kabab down on the plate and looked at Salil.

"What in the world is that? I'm sure you just made it up."

He held up his palms in a conciliatory gesture and then showed me his phone's screen.

"Don't trust me, trust Google. Cathisophobia is the fear of sitting at a desk, of being a desk jockey. You, my friend, are one of a dying breed. The real deal. The warrior. The one who goes out and does shit the rest of us wish we could. The one who still believes in good and evil and fighting the good fight. A total misfit in a world where people focus on creating the right perception on their bosses instead of what they actually do and edit and re-edit memos to make themselves look good and always try to cover their ass in case something goes wrong."

I watched him for a second. There was no mockery there. Just frank feedback from one friend to another. Then he grinned.

"What you suck at is trying to fit into an office. You are so miserable wearing that suit and typing reports."

"It's that obvious, is it?"

He laughed out loud.

"Sen, you have many talents and acting isn't one of them. Do you know why you're doing this? Why you agreed to the role Srini offered?"

I hadn't really thought about it, but when it came down to it, I owed Srini. He had done right by me. He had supported me when few people would. He had helped Ma get the experimental treatments that led to her recovery, and he had trusted my judgement when most bosses would have thought me crazy for accusing CIA agents we were working with of being part of a conspiracy to kill the US President. I told Salil that and he nodded.

"I get that, Sen but do you know why Srini has kept you doing this knowing how much you hate desk work?"

That stumped me. I had figured he needed work to

get done with Sean's death and he obviously trusted me. Salil answered his own question.

"Those days taught all of us that the days of officers running things wearing suits in the comfort of their offices were over. We bumped into an enemy which killed a senior Intelligence Bureau officer in his home and ambushed Srini's car and left him for dead."

"I know all that, man. What does that have to do with me?"

Salil winked.

"He's keeping you close because he trusts your ability to put such enemies in the ground when the time comes."

I thought about that. When we had been chasing down the assassins, I had been part of a task force that we had pulled together, one I had called Unit 22, paying homage to '22', the nickname given to the Special Frontier Force where I had spent so much of my career. It was telling that Srini had never officially disbanded it. Maybe Salil was right, and Srini had plans for me that extended beyond sitting at a desk and filling out reports.

Just then, my phone buzzed.

It was a message from Srini.

I have a job for you. See me first thing tomorrow morning.

***

"Aadi, now that you're posted in Delhi and have a stable office job, I'm sure you can meet some nice girl and settle down. Thirty is still young these days, but you really should think more seriously about it."

I put down my cup of coffee and glared at the old lady who seemed to have decided that her mission for the evening was to spoil my evening by giving me unsolicited advice on my love life. Ma saw the look in my eyes and coughed to get our attention.

"Rupa, I'll get some fresh pakodas. I had just put a batch in the pan. Come on and help me get them."

As they went to the kitchen, Ma turned towards me and smiled and winked. That was worth putting up with all kinds of advice from Rupa Aunty, my mother's cousin and notorious matchmaker extraordinaire, who had descended upon our home. She was in India ostensibly on a holiday from the US, where she lived with her son, but I suspected she had seen in me her latest project. She was staying with her daughter, who was married to a surgeon in Delhi, and she seemed to come over to our place more often than I would have liked. While the extended family didn't know what I did and what I had been through, they knew that my days of wearing a uniform, carrying a gun and field postings in godforsaken places were behind me and that I now did a respectable government job in the Home Ministry in Delhi. That was enough for Rupa Aunty to begin bombarding Ma with photographs and resumes of various girls in her network whose parents were looking for the perfect match.

Once Rupa Aunty had gone, I was in my room when Ma came in and sat on the bed next to me.

"How are you doing?"

"Work's okay, Ma."

She held my chin and turned my face towards her. To my men I had been an officer they would follow into harm's way, to my enemies I had been a foe they would regret facing, but to Ma, I was, and always would be her little boy, Aadi.

"I asked about you, not about your work. I hope Rupa's nagging didn't get to you."

She knew me and I knew her. I knew it wasn't the matchmaking that she was worried about getting to me, it was about how I was coping with Amy's death. She was right to worry. She had seen the nights when I had lain curled up in my bed, screaming in my nightmares, when I had confessed to wanting nothing more than to put a gun in my mouth and end it all. Ma had seen the best and the worst of me, and to her I could be nothing but honest.

"Ma, I miss Amy. I won't tell you otherwise, but earlier a loss like this would have made me want to end it all, to question whether life was worth living. Amy taught me that it was because there were people I could help. So, I'm hurting, but I'm learning to go on despite that. Perhaps that's the best one can do."

She tousled my hair and kissed my forehead.

The next morning, I was in Srini Iyer's office. Srini was the Additional Secretary, my boss. After Sean had died, Salil had been promoted into heading up Area One, the Pakistan desk, and I had been given charge of coordinating with the boys in the field, the operators in the SFF, one of whom I had been not so long ago. When Srini got up to shake my hand, I saw him limp slightly. None of us ever brought it up, but we knew that Srini had taken some permanent damage from the ambush he had barely survived. With a limp in his left leg and a right eye that would never get to full functionality, Salil thought that Srini would never rise to the top job in the intelligence fraternity. When I asked him why, he had said that at senior levels, it became all about optics, and the government wouldn't want the National Security Advisor looking anything less than fully fit. Also, Srini was good at what he did, but when it came to political savvy, he was outmatched by many of his peers. It was bullshit but it was the way the world worked. I knew that, Srini knew that, but the fact that he continued to drive himself as hard as ever made me respect him even more than I had previously, for it's a rare boss who works not for his personal advancement alone, but to try and make a difference.

"Sen, how are you dealing with the paperwork?"

For a panicked moment, I thought I had left out some details in that damned Form 42 or 43, or whatever it was.

"Sir, I'm learning. It's not as bad as I thought."

At that, he took off his glasses and laughed uproariously. Srini was a man not easily given to displays of emotion. On the rare occasion when he swore, which for him meant nothing more extreme than saying the f word, you knew things were horribly wrong. This was the first time I had seen him laugh like this, and I wondered what it presaged.

He motioned for me to sit down and pointed at the papers in front of him.

"Sen, these are your reports. Technically speaking, as your boss, I'd say you are not sticking to protocol. You are meant to summarize intel inputs from our boys, the Defense Intelligence Agency, the Intelligence Bureau and anything from relevant external assets and provide analysis. In three of the last four reports, you skipped some of the usual fields, but went on to add extra pages outlining tactical recommendations. That's not, strictly speaking, in your job description."

I was long used to getting shit for not doing my job in office well. Sean used to chew me out quite mercilessly. At least I hoped Srini would be decent and polite about it. I smiled and apologized, resolving to grin and bear it.

"You don't need to apologize, Sen."

That was a surprise, as Srini continued.

"The Special Group captain who led the raid against the Lashkar camp in Balakot sector sends his thanks.

The intel alone would not have told him to watch for Pakistani Special Services Group trainees nearby. Most desk-bound intel analysts would have missed them, focusing on active units. You saw that and guessed correctly that when the shit hit the fan, the Pakistanis would send them in to help."

"What happened, Sir? I hope our boys got out all right."

He nodded.

"They got out just fine. The poor SSG boys got roasted though. Our boys took out a dozen of them. Just kids really, starting off their training. You don't seem so happy at that, Sen."

Only someone who has gone into combat will understand how I felt. Sure, when you were engaged in combat, you were focused on winning and defeating the enemy. That didn't mean you hated them. They were just doing their jobs, trying to serve their flag. The SSG trainees would have been cannon fodder for my old buddies in the Special Group, especially since I had told them where they would come from. It wasn't the poor, stupid soldiers like me I hated, it was the political masters who sent us out to die for them. In this case, Pakistan had sacrificed a dozen good boys to protect some jihadi bastards they were breeding to send across the Line of Control.

"Well, Sen, I can see you're adding value here even though you hate sitting at a desk."

Once again. Was I so bloody obvious? Srini must have seen the expression on my face, and he laughed again.

"I can hear you massacring that keyboard from my cabin. So can everyone else around when you leave your door open."

Ouch. He smiled as he handed me a sheet of paper.

"What's this, Sir?"

His humor was gone, replaced by the steely glint of a career intelligence officer who had started life in the army.

"You've successfully completed your trial period."

What? I had been on a trial period?

"Sen, that paper has your new appointment. You are obviously an excellent field officer and someone whose instincts I trust. I needed to see whether you could survive in the office and work with the other agencies. I don't need you to like it, and I don't need you to be the best at it, I just need you to be able to tolerate it, which you've shown you can, and in fact, do it without losing your usual initiative."

"What do I do, Sir? What's the new appointment?"

"Sen, you were in the Special Group for a long time. What you and those boys do, even if most of it is never publicly known, saves lives and makes a difference. What the events of the last year showed us all was that our enemies aren't always across the border or in terror cells. We are dealing with dangerous enemies who can cut across the neat inter-departmental bifurcations we feel so comfortable with. I have been thinking of a new role for you, to not just continue liaising with the Special Group boys and intel agencies but when we spot complex threats, you'll be the one to pull together resources across us, the IB and the military to deal with it. I'm working on the proposal and will let you know when I get approval. Basically, I'm recommending that we make Unit 22 a full-time unit, reporting into me. Needless to say, I want you to head it. You pick your team, and if you want, Murthy can be transferred to work under you. I know you guys have been working very closely. You came up with the name, and you were the leader, with or without official designations, through all the chaos we dealt with a few months ago."

I began to smile and then he dashed my hopes.

"Sen, I really don't think you're going to get into ops again. You'll be sending in boys to do the job, not getting your hands dirty."

He could see the disappointment on my face, and he took on a more conciliatory tone.

"Sen, I'll be honest with you here. With the medals you've won and the visibility you've got in the media with all those awards, including the recent Ashoka Chakra, nobody would send you out to break heads again. Now I hear the US President has decided to award you for saving his life. Seems they're making up their mind what medal to give you but make room for it on your display case."

That was news to me. Many people did what they did in my line of work for medals and advancements. To be honest, I loathed my medals, because each of them came with memories of people I had lost. The US medal would forever be tainted by the memory of Amy's loss. Srini put another piece of paper in front of me.

"That doesn't mean I'm going to just have you sit at a desk and break that poor keyboard. I have a job for you."

I looked down at a black and white photograph of a balding man who was wearing glasses with a cigar dangling from his mouth.

"Do you know who this is, Sen?"

I had never seen the face and had no idea who this guy was, so Srini answered his own question.

"That is Danish Raza."

"The Danish Raza. The Mafia Don? The guy who once ruled Mumbai's underworld?"

Srini nodded.

"Looks nothing like him. He used to have more hair and was on the chubby side. Now that you mention it, the eyes look a bit familiar, but that's it."

"Lost hair, lost weight, seems he got a face job or a nose job to conceal his identity. We know he's been using an assumed identity for some time, and there have been all sorts of rumors about how he'd changed his face. Whatever the case, that's the man."

"Do you want me to kill him?"

I mean, when you've been in the line of work I have been in for so long, that's a perfectly natural question to ask. Especially when the man whose photo you're looking at is a gangster who has been accused of masterminding or financing terror strikes which ended up killing hundreds of people.

Srini laughed again, this time bringing Salil rushing into the room to check if everything was okay with the boss. For Srini to laugh so much in one morning was strange and would have been a welcome change from his normally serious demeanor had most of the laughter not been at my expense.

"Boss, are you okay?"

Srini looked at Salil and called him in, still chuckling.

"Murthy, come in and take a seat. You know what we're talking about.'

He then looked at me, and I saw that the dynamics in the room had shifted versus the past. I had never thought of me as anyone's boss, but Srini, having spent so much time in the corridors of bureaucracy, assumed he needed to explain why Salil knew of this before me, when he had just told me I was going to be Salil's boss.

"This intel came to Murthy through one of his contacts, so Murthy saw it. By the way, Murthy, I'm making Unit 22 official and permanent and promoting Sen to head it."

Salil congratulated me and then looked at the photo and Srini laughed again.

"Sen was asking if he finally gets to kill someone again when he saw the photo."

This time, Salil also joined in the laughter. I didn't see what was so funny about it, and then Salil enlightened me.

"We were chatting with your favorite minister this morning and when Srini mentioned to him that you were on the job, the first question he asked was whether you'd get worked up and kill Raza before getting him to India."

My favorite minister could only mean the honorable Manoj Kumar Pandey, the minister of state for Home Affairs, whom I had pissed off on a previous encounter. I have nothing against politicians as a group, but when they're as transparently corrupt and sleazy as Pandey, I find it hard to conceal my emotions. Sucking up to sleazy political bosses is perhaps right up there on my list of improvement areas along with typing. Then I remembered something I had heard once.

"Get him to India? Isn't he cooped up somewhere in Pakistan?"

Srini was all business again.

"Something's changed. Seems he was in Dubai attending a wedding and the Emirati authorities detained him for us."

"They'd do that, even if meant pissing off the Pakistanis?"

Srini had his hands steepled under his chin, as if enjoying the turn of events that had landed one of the most wanted men in India within arm's reach.

"They're pragmatic people. They can see they can make much more money off us, and the new foreign policy focus on strengthening strategic relations with them had to pay off sometime. Plus, I think the PM reminded them that they owe us."

"Owe us? How?"

Srini looked away, and I knew he was going to say something he wasn't terribly proud of.

"We caught a runaway princess for them a while ago."

I had read something about it in the papers. An Emirati princess had escaped, and the Indian government had brought her in, allowing Emirati special forces along with the Indian Coast Guard to catch her off the coast of Goa and send her back to what she claimed was a life of repression and abuse. To be honest, I had more sympathy for her than whatever political deals had justified the actions the government took at the time, but if it was netting us Raza, perhaps it had been worth it.

"Where is Raza now? Do I need to pull together a team to grab him?"

Salil chipped in.

"Nothing so exciting. The Emirati State Security Agency has him in custody in Dubai. You just need to babysit him and fly him back. The Emiratis will provide security there, and you'll be met by a bloody army at the airport here."

It didn't sound like much action, but sounded much more exciting than another week of filling out Form 42s, or were they 43s? On top of that, Raza was a certified grade-A asshole, responsible for bombings across India and funding many of the jihadis my buddies and I had killed in Kashmir. Even though I wasn't allowed to kill him, it would be sweet to deliver the bastard to justice, and then hope that he was hanged for all the lives he had taken and ruined.

"When do I start, Sir?"

Srini checked some papers in front of him and then looked up.

"You leave in two days. Should be a piece of cake, and you could use a break. Take a spare day in Dubai and relax for a change and then bring that son of a bitch here to face justice."

***

"Ma, I'll be gone for just three days. I don't need half the stuff you're putting in there."

Here I was, a thirty-year-old man, who had served in the army and done and seen all sorts of things, reduced to being ten years old again, heading off on a school trip, with my mother fussing over whether I had packed properly for the trip. Ma just glanced back at me and continued putting in the box of laddoos which she had made for me. Her laddoos had been my favorite sweets when I was growing up, and even when I had served in uniform, I had taken a box of them with me on my field postings. They never lasted very long, as my buddies ensured they were wolfed down within a day or two, but they reminded me of home, no matter where I was, and reminded me of Ma.

I sat down on the bed and watched her fuss over my bag and then it struck me that the last time she had made laddoos for me was before my last field posting to Kashmir, before my final mission, before the ambush that had nearly broken me. Well over a year and a half had passed since then, and in that period, I had fought my inner demons, then fought against deadly enemies who had killed many and even come after Ma, I had loved and lost Amy and most importantly, Ma had fought her own battle against cancer and won.

The laddoos she had made were not just a box of sweets. They showed that once again our lives were perhaps getting back to normal. I held Ma's hand, and she sat down next to me.

"Ma, you take care of yourself while I'm gone."

There was a sparkle in her eyes that I had not seen in a long time.

"While you're off enjoying Dubai, Rupa and I plan to catch up on some old Sean Connery DVDs."

Ma had long confessed to having a crush on Sean Connery. We had lost Baba when I had just been fifteen. He had served in the army as well, and with his passing, Ma and I had become more than mother and son. We were the best of friends, and a pillar of strength for each other.

"Ma, Salil had called me to talk about the trip, so don't wait up for me in case our meeting runs late."

She looked at me, a smile forming on the edge of her mouth.

"Don't drink too much. Your flight is early in the morning."

That was my Ma. She knew everything about me and loved me despite it all.

***

"There's this new analyst in the China desk who's pretty, and smart as well. Want to get introduced?"

I gave Salil a look he was long used to when he asked me that question. We were sitting at his home, sipping drinks, and he shrugged at me.

"Just trying to be a good friend and wingman. You do realize you can't be single the rest of your life."

I was about to protest when he held up his hands.

"Hey, I liked Amy a lot, but my friend, you do need to pick up the pieces of your personal life. I think Amy would have wanted you to be happy."

"I am happy."

No sooner had I said those words that I stopped myself. I was doing okay at work, and I was happy that Ma was recovering, but Amy's loss had left a hole which I still felt keenly. I wasn't sure anyone else could fill that or if I was ready. Salil poured me another drink.

"Sen, take your time. There's no rush, but you've been a soldier and you know this better than me. When you lose those you care about, you honor their memory but you carry on living."

I smiled and then, trying to deflect the conversation away from my messed up personal life, I asked him whether there would be any likely threat to be aware of when I was in Dubai. His response was interrupted as his eight-year-old son, Vihaan, ran into the living room, wearing pads, a helmet and carrying a bat.

"Daddy, I'm ready for the game."

Salil looked at me and winked.

"Champ, I can see you're ready, but your game is tomorrow morning. I suppose you won't want to sleep with all that on."

Vihaan looked at him and answered in all earnestness.

"Coach said that the more I wore them, the more I would be used to them. So, I will sleep with them on."

He then looked at me with his wide, eager eyes. I felt a stab of panic. I had fought Chechen mercenaries and Chinese commandoes, but I'd prefer to tangle with them versus handling a young, precocious child. If there was one thing I was worse at than typing reports in office, it was handling kids.

"Uncle, Daddy said that you like blowing things up. Is that true?"

I took a deep breath and glared at Salil before responding.

"Vihaan, I don't really like it. Sometimes it needs to be done."

He climbed up on the sofa next to me and looked up at me.

"That's cool. If I don't get into the Indian team, I'll be a commando."

I tousled his hair.

"I'm sure you'll get into the Indian team if you keep trying hard."

"Have you killed people?"

Shit. I had no idea how to answer that or what would be the age-appropriate way of telling a kid what a soldier sometimes had to do. Salil's wife, Bharathi, came to the rescue and shepherded Vihaan away, saying it was late for bed.

Salil's attention was back on me.

"Sen, you're overthinking this. There's no threat. Nobody knows they've agreed to hand over Raza. It's all being kept compartmentalized at the highest levels, and the Emiratis don't want any jihadis out for their blood if word gets out that they handed him over."

"Won't our media be all over it?"

Salil laughed and drained his bottle and picked another one up.

"Our media will know what the government wants it to know and when it wants them to know anything."

"What does that mean?"

"Here's the plan as far as I can understand it. You babysit that bastard over to India and we whisk him away to a safe house without anyone knowing about it. In a couple of weeks or so, by which time the spooks have drained all the intel they can get out of him, the government announces that our forces have captured him in a daring raid while he was at a safe house in Pakistan."

I put down my glass of rum.

"What the hell?"

Salil laughed and kept laughing as I kept staring at him.

"Sen, you should take a look at yourself. You still don't get how the politicians work, do you? Putting Raza away for life or stringing him up to hang is what he deserves, but no politician would miss milking such an opportunity. This way, the Emiratis are off the hook because nobody will know they handed him to us, we look good because we flexed our muscles and caught the bogeyman, and Pakistan looks bad because we say we caught him in a tribal area where they were harboring him."

I swore a few times under my breath. Words that I didn't want Vihaan to hear from the next room.

"Typical political bullshit, Salil. That's what it is."

He shrugged.

"You know how it goes. As long as it all serves a good purpose, and putting a specimen like Raza away is as good a purpose as one can think of. A big reason Srini is sending you is that he trusts you to keep it quiet. Sending a typical career bureaucrat who likes shooting his mouth off, or may be compromised, would risk the real story getting out."

I swore a few more times under my breath. I may not know how politicians thought and why they did what they did, but in my simple soldier's mind, I knew enough to know that when the fat politicians made complex self-serving plots, things usually went wrong. And the ones who did the dying and bleeding for them were stupid foot soldiers like me and my buddies. Salil poured me another drink.

"Have another one and we can raise a toast to you."

"To me?"

"Yeah. They'll need a hero or two as well, and the word is you'll get another medal. Supposedly for working the intel and plans to get Raza."

I slammed my glass down.

"I don't want another medal. Certainly not one I did nothing to earn."

Salil held my arm gently and looked into my eyes.

"My friend, some men spend all their lives trying to be heroes and never succeed. Others, like you, are born to be heroes but don't want the glory."

I shook my head, starting to say that I wasn't born to be a hero, that I hadn't wanted half the things to happen which led people to stick that tag on me, because they had meant the death of good men and women. Salil didn't let me finish.

"Sen, in the messed-up world we live in, those who are born to be heroes often have even more heroism thrust upon them by fat, corrupt bastards who want to use them for their own political purposes."

We both laughed at that, and I found some of my anger draining away. Yes, it would be yet another time when I would have been used by the political masters for their agenda, but it wouldn't be the first time a soldier was similarly screwed over and it wouldn't be the last.

"Salil, at least I'm happy we get Raza. I'll be so tempted to snap his neck."

He took a sip of his beer and smiled.

"Don't. He's a slimeball and in your shoes, I'd want to put a bullet in his head, but he is a treasure trove of intel. Once we have him, we can learn all about his connections with the Pakistani Inter-Services Intelligence. He could help us bust a whole bunch of other ISI ops."

I knew that. Srini's mission brief had been crystal

clear on that count but that just made it even more frustrating. I mean, the Americans didn't bother to get Osama back and feed him biryani for years while he awaited trial. They blew his fucking head off, but orders were orders. Salil's grin had widened, and I knew he was up to no good.

"What are you smiling at?"

"You do realize what you'll have to do when you come back, don't you?"

"What?"

"Fill up a Form 42 about the mission, and this time I'm pretty sure they won't accept any missing fields. Lots of big bosses will want to see the report."

I swore loudly as Salil burst out laughing.

***

EPISODE TWO

BEAUTY & THE BABOON

"Good morning, Rupa Aunty. I hope you're well."

I had to keep a straight face and force a smile. These were the moments when you hated modern technology. I had been ambushed into accepting a FaceTime call moments after my flight landed in Dubai. Seeing that the call was from Ma, I obviously accepted, but when the call connected, I saw Rupa Aunty on the screen. Ma was in the background, and she smiled and gave an exasperated shrug of her shoulders.

"Aadi, you're in Dubai!"

In addition to being a pesky matchmaker, Rupa Aunty had a firm grasp of the obvious. Of course, that was another thing I couldn't tell her, so I just nodded silently.

"What are you doing now? Are you busy?"

Well, the truth was that I had woken up at six in

the morning to catch my flight. The slight hangover from the previous night's drinking hadn't helped and any hopes of sleeping the hangover off on the flight were dashed by the snoring, obese diamond merchant sitting next to me. To be honest, I had no idea what he did, but the bracelets, necklaces and rings he had on made him look like a walking jewelry showroom.

"Aadi, you aren't saying much. Look, I have some urgent work for you. I need you to get something for me from Dubai."

I took a deep breath. Such sentences from Rupa Aunty, as I had discovered over the last few months, were usually succeeded by an email with a girl's photograph. I felt like hanging up and hurrying up so I wouldn't get caught up in a long queue at immigration and then get to my hotel and sleep. Instead, I smiled and asked her what I could do for her.

"So sweet of you. Some girl will be so lucky to be married to you. In fact, I may know a couple whose parents recently got in touch with me."

Seeing that the conversation was veering off dangerously back into matchmaking territory, I quickly brought it back on track. Better to be an errand boy for Rupa Aunty than to subject myself to more of her matchmaking.

"Aunty, just tell me what you need. My meeting's tomorrow morning. Today I really am pretty free."

She beamed in delight, an expression that began

with her mouth and quickly cascaded through all her three chins. As you can see, I was struggling to remain civil and focused and hoped she would quickly get to what she wanted. She held up her own phone and I saw a strange photo on it. I had to look twice to make sure it was what it seemed to be.

A baboon holding a bulb. A fucking baboon holding a bulb.

I wasn't that hungover, so I couldn't have been imagining it and as Rupa Aunty's face came back on camera, my smile was back.

"Aadi, one of my friends back in LA had these at her lamps at her home. So adorable, isn't it? She had a whole set of them. One standing up straight like the one I showed you, one sitting down, one hanging from the wall. So adorable, and she had got them in Dubai."

Oh no. This was worse than a Form 42. She wanted me to buy a whole troop of baboons carrying bulbs. I was good at some things, but acting wasn't one of them, and there were limits to how far I could carry on my obedient and polite nephew act. My expression must have showed how I felt, and I could see Rupa Aunty immediately look concerned and her voice was apologetic.

"I know you're there on work, but please get me one of these. They're available at the Galleries Lafayette at Dubai Mall."

Ma was scowling in the background, instant feedback for my lapse of politeness, and I got my smile back.

"Sure, Aunty, I'll get a baboon."

Now, it was Rupa Aunty's turn to scowl.

"That's not a baboon, Aadi. That is a macaque."

Whatever. If it looked like a baboon, it was a baboon to me. Add primatology to the list of things I sucked at. Ma grinned in the background and told me she'd call me later as we hung up.

I had reached immigration when I was pleasantly surprised to see a familiar face near the immigration counter. Ankit Sharma. The Intelligence Bureau officer who had worked with me in tracking down the assassins six months earlier. The last time I had seen him, he had been taking on three terrorists carrying AK-47s, armed with nothing but a revolver. I had spotted in him a capable agent early on, but that night, he had become a bona fide hero in my books. He looked like an accountant, thin, slightly stooped, with a receding hairline and wearing glasses, but in the real world, the ones who tried too hard to look like heroes were usually fakes. Real heroes didn't wear capes or have six packs, they just did what was right even when it meant swimming against the tide.

Sharma grinned when he saw me and extended his hand for me to shake. I shocked him by hugging him.

"Man, it's good to see you, and good to see you here. I never got a chance to meet you afterwards. They said you were on a long leave to recover, but you saved my life that night."

Sharma looked sheepishly down.

"Major, I got assigned to the Embassy in Abu Dhabi just a month ago."

The man standing next to Sharma smiled and introduced himself.

"Major Sen, I am Captain Emad Abu Sharekh from the State Security Agency. I'll be your liaison here."

Sharekh looked competent and from his straight bearing, firm grip, and solid build, I guessed he might be a spook now, but he had been a soldier at one time like me. Sharekh took my papers, and we breezed through immigration and were outside within minutes. I could see Sharekh and Sharma chatting amiably, and it struck me then that India and the UAE must have been very tight on the intel front if the SSA knew the IB man at the Embassy and one of their officers was openly chatting with him like old friends.

"Where are you going, Major?"

I looked at Sharekh, a bit puzzled.

"I was just trying to see where the taxi queue is. I'm booked at the Bonnington."

Sharekh tut-tutted and shook his head gently.

"That is a decent hotel, Major, but my bosses had you upgraded, and you don't need a taxi."

Soon a black SUV came up and Sharma and I got into the back, Sharekh insisting that as the host, he ride in the front with the driver, who was a very large, bearded man. As we drove through the city, my first time in Dubai, two things struck me. I had read about how Dubai had been created in the middle of a desert, but seeing the gleaming, modern metropolis with my own eyes was something else. Second, getting anywhere in Dubai perhaps took half the time it would take in Delhi over the same distance. The traffic was better, but the roads were what made the difference. I had never been one for doing touristy things, so I didn't pay much attention to the tall buildings and famous landmarks the magazine on the plane had insisted I check out. I had been to Israel, Singapore and a bunch of other places for training and exercises when I had served, but I had been focused on learning from other warriors, being quickly branded as the boring boss by my men, who were keen to check out the local brew and women with perhaps as much zeal as learning about Sayeret Matkal tactics. In actual ops, I had been to more exotic places in Tibet and others I could never tell anyone about, but on those trips, I had been too busy trying to keep from getting killed to worry about sightseeing.

"We're here."

I stepped out of the SUV, assuming that Sharekh's bosses had upgraded me to a better hotel. I hadn't reckoned on being upgraded into a bloody beach resort- the Le Meridien resort. As we walked inside, the manager came up and shook my hand and began to tell me of the multiple restaurants, the private beach and other facilities, which I was sure never to use. I took Sharma aside for a second.

"Isn't this all too much? I mean, I shouldn't be here. This must be costing a bomb."

Sharma laughed out aloud.

"Sen, almost every government officer I know would give his right arm to come on a junket like this and live it up on the government's dime, and they go and choose the one officer who doesn't give a damn and wants to save the government money."

Sharekh must have overheard, for he too smiled and came up to me.

"Major, I'm happy to see am honest soldier in a world of crooked politicians."

From what little I knew of Emirati politics and government, that took serious balls for a serving officer to say and raised Sharekh several notches in my eyes.

"This is not just for the luxury. The man you are here to take back is staying in this resort as well, so it makes the logistics easier."

That took a few seconds to sink in. Raza was staying here? I had pictured him in a government safe house, if not in prison. Sharekh grinned again.

"He's in the biggest suite, courtesy of his friends in the royal family. We are sending him off but want to make sure he doesn't complain about not being treated well."

I should have figured that the biggest crooks would be staying in the fanciest suite in a resort like this. That's the kind of world we unfortunately lived in. Sharekh shook my hand and began to leave.

"Major, we will meet Mr. Raza late tonight, and your flight is tomorrow afternoon. We will also get some time together to understand the logistics in a briefing tomorrow morning. Till then, please enjoy your stay in Dubai."

As he walked off, Sharma tapped me on the shoulder.

"You look like you could use some rest. How about I pick you up in the evening and we grab a drink? Then we can meet our friendly Don."

"Yeah, that sounds good. I need to go to the Dubai Mall. Why don't you pick me up there?"

"Shopping?"

My response left Sharma visibly flabbergasted.

"Yeah, I need to buy a baboon."

***

In my limited time in Dubai, I managed to figure out that whoever planned the place had a simple mantra.

If in doubt, make it big. No, actually, make it huge.

The buildings were tall, and to be honest some were pretty over the top, like a hotel shaped like an Egyptian pyramid, complete with hieroglyphs. However, if I thought I had seen big, Dubai Mall redefined that word for me. The place looked like a small city with an aquarium, an ice-skating rink, and a seemingly endless procession of luxury boutiques. They were all wasted on me. I didn't buy luxury brands, both because I thought it stupid to spend so much money on a wallet or shoe, and more pragmatically because my government salary meant they were pretty out of my budget. I didn't skate and I had no interest in fish unless it was being served to me on a plate. So, I wandered around, getting lost several times, discovering that I had taken a full circuit of the floor, passing a bloody full-sized dinosaur fossil, and arrived back where I had started.

Why would they put a full-sized dinosaur in a mall? Again, when in doubt, make it big. I could see no other logic for it. I almost bumped into a large, bearded Arab man wearing flowing white robes. He scowled at me, and I apologized and then a pretty, blond tourist wearing a short dress bumped into me. She offered an apology, and I told her none was needed.

As I watched her walk past, I noticed several women, probably tourists, dressed as they would in any other big city, and a group of loud Russian women wearing really short skirts. The tourist guide I'd skimmed through on the plane had mentioned something about women needing to dress modestly in Dubai. Clearly these women hadn't got the memo, or the definition of modest was different here. I wasn't complaining- it made for better viewing than fish in a tank or kids slipping on ice.

I asked one of the Russians, out of pure coincidence the prettiest one, what and where Galleries Lafayette was. She smiled charmingly and then looked at me blankly. Then a lightbulb seemed to go off somewhere in her head and she pointed right. I meandered along that direction for a while and then, hopelessly lost, asked a big, bearded Arab. He guided me to a touchscreen information kiosk and showed me exactly where it was.

Just another example of how in the world we live in, unfortunately what looks good is often not good for you.

I reached the fancy department store and was staring at the baboons holding lamps when a lady came up to me.

"Sir, these are exquisite. Very popular. How many would you like?"

"Just one. Look, I need to take it with me to India, so can you pack it in a way that I could check it in?"

She looked horrified at the suggestion.

"We could, Sir, but if you ask me, it's highly risky. These are sturdy pieces but with very fine workmanship. Each piece has a solid metal core around which the ceramic is put, but the way those baggage handlers toss luggage around, they may bend something. Just last week, we had a loyal customer from the US who complained that one of their lamps arrived broken."

I wondered if that was Rupa Aunty's friend and

then picked the sitting baboon, judging that it would be the smallest and easiest to take through as an added item of hand baggage. She covered up the baboon in a transparent plastic cover with some bubble wrap, and most of him was concealed, but his bloody face was sticking out, as if mocking me.

Ten minutes later, I walked out of the shop, cursing my luck and Rupa Aunty. The government had given me an underworld don as a travel companion. She had added a bloody baboon to that list.

***

I had a quick lunch at the food court inside the Galleries Lafayette, where a bit to my surprise, they were serving Indian food. I skipped that and ordered some pasta and drank a beer. There had to be some perks to having a day off in Dubai and if I was going to spend my day with a baboon and the evening with a don, I might as well get a little buzzed.

Sharma had messaged me that he was caught up at work and instead of picking me up at the Dubai Mall, would meet me back at the hotel. I didn't mind. It gave me time to have one more beer with my new baboon pal. I patted the baboon on his head.

"Just you and me, buddy. Just you and me. Come, let's get back to the hotel."

I FaceTimed Ma and she laughed out loud as I

showed her the baboon.

"You are going soft, Aadi. I didn't think you'd actually get that for Rupa. She'll be so thrilled."

"Yeah, maybe then she'll go easy on the matchmaking front for a while."

It was good to see Ma laugh again. Both Ma and I had fought our own demons and we had both barely scraped through. That shared experience had brought us even closer, if such a thing was possible.

Now began my meandering path back to where I could get a taxi, since I had no idea about how to get there in the labyrinth of a mall which had clearly been designed to entrap people like me. Past lessons learned well, I ignored all the attractive tourists and looked around for a local.

"Mama, that man is also carrying a monkey. Why did you say I shouldn't carry George as he'd look strange?"

I looked down to my left and saw a little boy, perhaps five or six years old, though to be honest, my judgement in how old kids are or how tall they should be, is hardly reliable. Great, so now people would make fun of me carrying my bloody baboon along. The kid was carrying a stuffed monkey- again, not being a primatologist, I mentally tagged it as a chimp, wearing a red t-shirt. The kid stuck the chimp out towards me.

"Say hello to Georgie. What's your monkey's name?"

The kid seemed to have a British accent. Perhaps lived there and had come to visit relatives or something. He had big eyes, dimples, curly hair and a few teeth missing. Someone more given to such matters may have thought him cute. I just thought he and the chimp were made for each other.

"Hey Georgie. My baboon doesn't have a name yet. I just got it."

The kid scowled, and then examined me with an intense expression.

"That's a macaque, not a baboon."

Fuck. Everyone seemed to know that except me. Then I had a flash of inspiration.

"Her name is Rupa."

That seemed to satisfy the kid and his mom tugged at his hand to pull him along.

"Come on, Amir."

Another British accent. I had met some Brits in my time, most of them SAS troopers we had trained with. From what I'd learned from them and how the ordinary trooper spoke compared to some of their officers, her accent was definitely what they would have called posh. Then another flash of inspiration struck me. Chances were that this lady would know much more about the mall than me.

"Excuse me, ma'am, how do I get to the taxi stand?"

She seemed to hesitate and then turned towards me. It was a bit disconcerting speaking to someone whose eyes you could not see. The rest of her body was totally covered in black, and even her eyes were covered by a black mesh.

"You go the floor that has the ice rink. There's a fountain there. You can't miss it because it has these statues of people diving into it. Just next…"

Then she froze and abruptly turned away, pulling the kid along.

"Hey, mom, you're hurting my hand!"

But she wasn't looking at me or her son. She was looking past me. I followed her gaze and saw three large men, all wearing track suits. One was a big, bald brute with a shaggy beard, and the other two were smaller copies of him with hair. All were wearing what seemed to be identical track suits. Members of some heavyweight wrestling team, brothers who liked shopping for sports apparel together or hired muscle whose bosses bought their clothes in bulk.

Whoever they were, they were not my business.

My old boss, Sean, used to keep saying that one of my biggest problems was my inability to keep my nose out of other people's business. That instinct for self-preservation which perhaps came naturally to people who had spent their lives navigating a bureaucratic career however clashed with all the values my parents had taught me and what I had learned in the army. We existed to protect those who couldn't protect themselves. If that meant putting others' safety ahead of our own, so be it.

They never said it aloud, but I suspect Sean and others like him would have thought someone like me naïve or just plain stupid. Well, stupid and naïve people died on your behalf so you wouldn't have to pick up a gun and go defend what was ours.

I took a deep breath. There I was going off the rocker again. Once again, getting worked up into doing something that would get me into trouble and totally fuck up my mission. The three men were probably just harassing the lady and would no doubt move on to do whatever louts like them did in a mall like this. I began to walk off and then I caught one of the smaller men look towards the parking exit. He motioned to the big guy who looked at the exit and grinned.

The woman and kid I had just met were going out the exit and looked like these three were interested in more than just some casual stalking. The big man caught me looking at the exit and when I turned my head, I found myself looking straight into his eyes. I had seen such eyes many times in my life.

He was no wrestler, big brother with a domineering sense of fashion or a small-time goon.

He was a killer.

None of my fucking business.

I kept telling myself that and began to walk away. I was here on an official trip, which I could not fuck up. Getting Raza was a big deal. We had been after him for decades and getting him to justice was more important than interfering with some thugs out to harass a lady in Dubai. The security briefing the boys in office had given me had been quite unambiguous. No guns, no trouble. Keep a low-profile, get Raza, and get back.

That's all I needed to do.

That's all I was going to do.

I kept walking and registered through my peripheral vision all three men starting to run towards the exit.

Don't do it.

Keep walking.

I remembered the man's eyes.

The little kid.

The posh accent.

Those three brutes.

With the way they reacted to spotting the woman and the way they ran after her, they weren't just looking to pass a casual comment while walking past her in the mall.

Keep walking.

Then I stopped. Screw it all. Screw all the idiots who pretended to tell people what to do or not to do sitting in their air-conditioned cocoons. In the real world, there were wolves out there, and occasionally they needed to be put down. For better or worse, that was one of the few things I was good at. No way would I walk away and leave that woman to be assaulted and perhaps raped in front of her kid.

I took a deep breath and looked at the baboon in my hand.

"Come on buddy, we're going to get into some big trouble."

***

"Georgie will beat you up. Don't touch my Mama!"

I wouldn't have known where to look among all the parked cars had I not heard the kid scream at the top of his voice. I ran towards the voice and saw something I'll never forget. The woman was backed up against a van and in front of her stood the kid, holding the chimp out defiantly at the three men. The big guy laughed.

"Get the fuck out of the way, kid."

He tossed the kid aside and he careened into me. I caught him, and still holding onto him, faced the three men.

"He's more of a man than any of you, but why don't you pick on someone your own size?"

The big guy looked at me, his brain perhaps processing where he had seen me before.

"Mister, mind your own business. Go."

I held out my hands, wide, in a universal gesture of not wanting trouble. I hope he got that meaning even though I had a bloody baboon lamp in my right hand.

"Just let the lady and the kid come with me and I'll go right now."

One of the lackeys whispered something to the big guy and he growled at him, sending him scurrying back a step. There was no doubt who was in charge of this merry band, and also who was smarter. The bigger guy may have been the boss, but the lackey was smarter. He had wanted de-escalation, and if they had agreed, I would have liked nothing more than to walk away. The big guy turned his neck left and right, and I could hear popping noises. Very impressive, but did this guy think that would intimidate me? Since we couldn't just stand there all day and make popping noises with our joints to impress each other, I took a step towards the lady.

"Please come with me, ma'am."

She took my hand without hesitation and was coming towards me when I felt a paw on my chest. The big guy had stepped towards me and was shoving me back. He was big, with at least three or four inches of height on me, and I'm not a small guy, standing nearly six feet. He also had a few kilos on me, though a lot of that seemed to have gone into his gut. He was strong, but even more overpowering than his strength was his bad breath. If it came to a fight, it wasn't certain I would prevail. There were three of them, and I had no real idea of their capabilities or whether they were armed. I needed to act, and act first.

When I had been a kid, I had possessed a ferocious temper, forever getting into scrapes. My father had made me learn Karate to try and channel that aggression and to teach me some discipline. I got a Black Belt by the time I finished school. Karate was great, and I learned a lot, but the army made me unlearn some of it. For one, when you do the things I did in uniform, you don't believe in the concept of fair fights, you take every advantage you can. You don't fight to defend yourself; you fight to kill the guy who's trying to kill you. Finally, you don't fight unarmed. If anything, you use every single conceivable weapon you can that's at hand. I've once battered a terrorist to death with a kettle. We were in a house in Kashmir, where he had holed up and surprised me when I went in on a search op. Our scuffle took us to the kitchen where we used knives, bare hands and at one point, he actually took a swing at me with a pot. I guess that saying about the pot and the kettle takes on a whole new dimension when you've seen the shit I have.

But I digress.

Big bald guy pushing me.

Left hand holding lady's hand.

Right hand holding baboon.

I moved my right hand up sharply, in a near vertical motion, and the head of the baboon, metal core, ceramic and all, made solid contact with the bald guy's jaw. Being hit on the jaw can be pretty tough on anyone. Being hit by a metal baboon can make that infinitely worse. When you hit someone hard enough on the jaw, his head quickly accelerates around. After a fraction of a second, it quickly decelerates as muscles, tendons, and bones prevent the head from spinning any further by providing an opposite force of equal magnitude. Newton's laws of motion and all that, you know. The poor brain inside floats in a fluid and while the head's spinning back and forth, the brain is slamming into the sides of the skull. Neurotransmitters fire, nervous system overloads and you go unconscious.

That would have been bad enough, but I wanted to put the leader out for good, so I let go of the lady's hand, grabbed baldy's shoulders, and head butted him. Between a broken nose, a smashed jaw and a damaged brain, he clearly had his set of issues and as he staggered back, I kicked him hard in the nuts. That proved to be the last straw and he collapsed soundlessly.

So far, the score read: baboon one, bad guys zero.

Seeing their boss go down, one of the minions came at me with some fancy kick with his right leg which might have been impressive in a dojo or in a low budget martial arts flick. He had trained well, but obviously had never fought someone who was trained to kill. Trying fancy high kicks in a real street fight, especially against someone with serious training does two things. One, it makes you look cool for the second or two when your leg is raised at an impressive angle. Two, it puts you down on the ground so fast you have no time to bask in that short-lived coolness.

I took a short, shuffling step to my right, pivoted my body slightly and caught his leg with my left hand, leaving him standing on one leg, looking a bit like an idiot. I swung the baboon like a club, landing three blows in quick succession to his head. The first took him on the left ear and he howled. I brought my hand back on the reverse swing, striking him just below the right ear and the final blow was an uppercut that smashed into his jaw, knocking out a tooth or two. The coup de grace was me stepping in slightly with my left foot, turning my body a bit to the left and then striking out with my right foot in a kick which broke his tibia. He went down in a heap, screaming all kinds of unintelligible shit in Arabic.

Baboon two, bad guys zero.

The third guy in a show of misplaced bravado or loyalty towards his fallen brethren, launched himself at me. I have no idea what exactly he wanted to do. Maybe he fancied his wrestling skills and wanted to get me down to the ground and grapple with me. I had no time for this shit. I pivoted my body, taking it out of the line of his attack, caught his right hand with mine in a lock and brought the baboon down hard on the nape of his neck as he passed me. He went down and forward, his head smashing into a parked car.

Baboon three, bad guys zero.

I turned to the lady.

"Let's get out of here now!"

I grabbed the lady's hand, she caught her son's hand, and we ran back into the mall. I had no idea what came next. The cops might come looking for us after seeing the mayhem in the mall CCTV cameras or the louts might have friends who'd be looking for revenge. Either way, we needed to get out of there. We ran more than walked to the elevator and went down to the floor where the taxi queue was, and I don't think I took a breath till we were in front of the taxis.

"Where are you going?"

The woman just looked at me. We didn't have time to waste. I could just imagine goons, cops or both coming for us.

"Let me know where you need to go, and I'll ask the cabbie to take you there."

She held my arm.

"Please take us with you."

Strange request, but then I was having a strange day, and I had no more time to waste, so we got into a cab, and I asked the driver to take us to my hotel. As the taxi began to drive away, I took a deep breath and looked back at the woman and the kid in the back seat. It was hard to see how the lady was coping with things, since her face was covered but then she spoke.

"Thank you. I really mean it. If you hadn't come, they would have killed us."

What struck me were not the words, but the fact that despite all that had just happened, her voice was even, without a trace of panic. The kid was looking at me with wide eyes.

"You're like Van Damme and your monkey is so

strong. Too bad about him."

I looked down at the baboon.

Its head was smashed, the metal showing from under the cracked skull, one arm was missing and there was blood all over its head and neck. That explained why the driver had been looking at me in a funny way from the moment I had stepped into the cab.

I put my head back against the seat.

I had been given a few, simple things to do on my first day in Dubai. Basically, I had to rest, sleep, not get into any trouble and buy a baboon. I had managed to mess even that up.

For a moment, I thought I'd be happier typing another Form 42.

Then on second thoughts, no, beating up three goons with a baboon was much more satisfying. I grinned as we drove towards the hotel and to whatever else lay in wait for me on a day I had messed up so spectacularly.

***

I dumped the baboon in a garbage can before we reached the hotel, and I gave a fat tip to the taxi driver. I wasn't sure if he would call the cops or not, but once I was in the hotel, I would call Sharma and get his help to figure things out.

Once we reached my room, I settled the kid down

on the sofa and handed him a juice from the mini bar and asked him if he wanted anything to eat.

"A pizza, some fries and a Coke."

I looked at his mother to see if she was okay with her son overdosing on junk food and her answer shocked me.

"We haven't eaten in a day. So please get him what he wants. I'll compensate you later."

I placed the order and give the kid a chocolate bar from the mini bar and went to the bathroom to clean up. I looked in the mirror and was surprised to see blood splatters on the side of my face and my nose. No wonder the taxi driver had been so spooked. I had been really lucky no cop had grabbed me at the mall itself. I washed my hands and face and as I was drying my face, I saw the lady at the bathroom door behind me. After what she'd been through she seemed to be holding up quite well. As I went back into the room, the kid, displaying the amazing short-term memory of young kids, was playing with George and jumping on the sofa. I kicked off my shoes and sat on the bed.

I was woken up by the sound of the phone ringing.

"Sir, the food you ordered is there. Could you please open the door."

Damn. I had fallen asleep. The kid was sitting on the sofa, giggling as he looked at me. The mom seemed to still be in the bathroom. I opened the door and as the room service guy laid out the food, the kid started digging into the pizza. The bathroom door opened and out stepped a young woman wearing a black dress. I stared at her; a bit gobsmacked. I had been expecting the burqa-clad lady. The woman in front of me was quite possibly the most beautiful woman I had ever seen, with her chiseled features, long hair that came down to the middle of her back, piercing blue eyes and a black dress that clung to the curves of her body.

She must have sensed how I felt so she smiled, holding up the burqa which she was now carrying in her hands.

"Much more comfortable this way."

She walked to me and offered her hand for me to shake.

"I'm Aisha. Thank you for helping us."

I was conscious that I was standing there with my mouth open, but it took me a second or two to recover.

"I'm Aaditya. Please eat something."

While they ate, I asked Aisha if I could help get her home. She looked up at me, a French fry in her hand, and as she paused to speak, Amir grabbed it and ate it, earning a frown from his mother and a smile from me.

"Mister Aaditya, we have a flight to catch early tomorrow morning and we have nowhere safe to go. Is it okay if we stay with you till our flight?"

That was a request I had not been ready for. I had jumped in to help them on impulse and had assumed that she would be on her way to her home, hotel or wherever else she needed to go. I glanced at my watch. It was past four in the evening. Sharma would show up soon, then Sharekh would come, and we were expected to meet Raza. How the hell was I going to manage all that with this woman and kid in my room?

"I'm really sorry, ma'am, but I'm here on a business trip and my colleague will be arriving shortly. So, I can't really be here very long."

"Can we then just stay in your room?"

I paused before answering. That was a strange request, but this lady was clearly in some trouble.

"Where are you flying, ma'am?"

"Toronto. Our flight is at one thirty in the morning, and we'll leave by eleven. I just don't want to be outside till then. After what happened at the mall, I don't feel safe."

I had many questions to ask, such as who she was and why she didn't feel safe anywhere other than the hotel room of a total stranger whom she'd met less than an hour ago. As it turned out, I didn't have to say anything. She looked at me imploringly, holding my hand in hers.

"Sir, I really am in some trouble, and I don't know where else to go. I don't want to impose on you and would hate for you to get involved any more than you need to, but I don't know where else to go and who else to turn to."

"Ma'am, you don't even know me."

She looked me straight in the eye.

'I know that you put yourself in danger to save

a complete stranger and her son. Nobody does that nowadays. Most people would have walked away and a few idiots I know would have taken a video and put it on social media. What you did tells me all I need to know about you.'

The kid piped up, his mouth half full of pizza.

"He saved Georgie and I think he's actually Van Damme."

The woman once again got my attention by gently squeezing my hand.

"Sir, please. Please let us stay here till we can leave for the airport."

Maybe she was very persuasive, maybe she acted very well, maybe she was genuinely in deep trouble and needed help, maybe I was too tired to argue, or maybe I was a sucker for beautiful women. Perhaps, truthfully, a combination of all those reasons. Either way, I found myself nodding.

Next thing I knew, Georgie was on my lap and the kid was hugging me.

My phone buzzed. It was a message from Sharma.

Am at the hotel. Coming up to your room.

How was I going to explain to him that I had picked up extra baggage in the form of a beautiful woman, a little kid, and a stuffed monkey?

***

EPISODE THREE

THE DON

I caught Sharma just as he exited the elevator on my floor. If he was surprised at seeing me waiting for him, he didn't say anything. I figured it was best for all concerned that he not know about the new guests I had picked up who were waiting in my room.

"Sharma, why don't we grab a drink at the bar?"

'Good idea. They have a nice poolside bar, and Raza will come to sit at the beach in a while and you can meet him. Sharekh should also be here by then."

I didn't say anything, but Raza's stay here seemed more and more like a holiday than imprisonment. When we had got a beer each, I asked Sharma what the deal was. He grinned and took a big swig.

"It is a bit absurd, but it's the way it is. Raza has to be treated well here because to do anything else would reflect poorly on the sheikhs whom he has supported in the past."

What sheikhs? Another big swig later, Sharma continued.

"He's no longer just a small-time underworld don. He was in deep with the Pakistani military leadership, funding some of their dirty work, helping move men and material where they wanted using his smuggling roots."

"So why did the Pakistanis throw him out? I gather he was staying there like royalty for many years."

Sharma rolled his eyes.

"These guys are like a pit of snakes. You never know who will bite you. From what I gather, the Pakistanis didn't move him. He came to Dubai to avoid being killed by the ISI."

I raised my eyebrows and stared at him. Killed by the ISI? Whatever for? Wasn't he one of their team?

Sharma drained his beer and called for another.

"There's no concept of loyalty among snakes like them. The Pakistanis were under pressure from us and the Americans to hand over wanted fugitives, and with their economy in deep shit, they were keen to avoid any more blacklists. They would never hand over someone like Raza. He knows too many of their secrets. They would probably just tell the world he died of a heart attack or kidney failure."

I saw where this was going.

"No doubt, a heart attack or kidney failure caused by a single bullet to the back of the head."

Sharma laughed.

"Now you're beginning to understand how these snakes work."

"So, what's with the sheikhs?"

Sharma took another large swig. I was quickly learning that keeping pace with him drink for drink would leave me wasted so I left my mug on the table, taking a breather, while he finished half his mug, wiped the foam off his mouth and continued.

"He used to spend a lot of time here back in the good old days of the underworld, investing in all sorts of things, doing arms deals and bankrolling movies. He did a lot of favors for some local sheikhs and they won't easily forget what they owe him. The government here wants to be rid of him, so they are passing him on to us as a token of goodwill, but he has enough connections to ensure he's treated very well and loses no face while he's here."

He stopped speaking and looked past me.

"Speaking of the devil, he's here."

I turned to see Sharekh walking towards us. Behind him were two large men in black suits and wearing wraparound black sunglasses. Clearly the muscle to guard the man walking next to Sharekh.

I remembered the news about the bomb explosions and the terror plots Danish Raza had orchestrated, and part of me wanted to run up to him and snap his neck. I think Sharma saw the expression in my eyes and put a hand gently on my shoulder.

"Major, someone else will be judge, jury and executioner if needed."

I kept glaring at the man walking towards us, bare-chested, wearing shorts, carrying a cocktail glass in his hand. His body was pretty toned despite his age, which was supposed to be well over sixty, and together with his rimless glasses, made him look more like a wealthy businessman on holiday rather than a wanted man about to face imprisonment or execution. Sharekh greeted me and I got up to shake his hand, my eyes never leaving Raza.

As the two of them sat down, Sharekh ordered a Coke for himself and Raza took a sip of his cocktail, before putting his glass on the table. His hands were neatly manicured and delicate looking, the hands of a man used to a life of comfort. He had started his career in the alleyways of Mumbai, shooting rival gangsters. Clearly, life in hiding had been good to him.

"Is this the young man who will accompany me to Mumbai?"

When Sharekh nodded, Raza put his hand out. I hesitated for a second and then shook it. His hand was soft and squishy, and I squeezed a bit harder than I needed to. He held my gaze and smiled.

"Not a bureaucrat, for sure. Not even a cop. I'd say you were in the army."

I didn't say anything back as he smiled and took

another sip of his drink.

"What's your name, young man?"

"Sean D'Silva."

That was my old boss. I saw no reason to give a lowlife, especially a dangerous lowlife like Raza, my real name. He once had a reputation for sending his goons after officers who were honest enough or stupid enough to come after him despite his political connections and riches. He grinned as he took another sip.

"I read D'Silva died. No matter. Once you're comfortable with me, you can tell me your real name. We have the whole flight to spend together, so we may as well get to know each other a bit."

That surprised me. He was supposedly a man on the run, yet he was connected enough or aware enough to know what had happened to an officer like Sean. He smiled at me appraisingly.

"Good height, good build, decent face. You could try your luck at the movies. Am sure you'll get the action roles naturally. They may have to work on the dancing."

He laughed and I wanted to knock his teeth out there and then.

"No thank you, Mr. Raza. I am perhaps better than you in my career choices. I don't pick dead end careers."

He raised his glass in a toast which I didn't bother reciprocating. Sharekh cut in, reminding me that the purpose of this meeting was to go through all the security protocols for the next day. That took almost an hour, and then Sharma and Sharekh left, telling me they would be at the hotel by nine in the morning to prep for our trip to the airport. Sharekh told me that he had given my number to the guards in case they needed to coordinate with me and gave me their numbers. In passing he winked.

"The chances of you needing to call them is zero. Nothing exciting will happen, but it's part of the protocol."

The two guards saluted when Sharekh left and were clearly there to ensure Raza didn't loiter and went back to his room. I asked them if I could buy them anything to eat or drink, and they shook their heads. Raza smiled at me.

"You would have been a good officer. Not too many people care about guards like them or the work they do. In my time leading men of my own, I realized the key to generating followership was to watch for the little guy, the ones down the chain, who otherwise would go ignored. Watch out for them, understand them and they will follow you, and the others will follow you, knowing that you look after even the little guy."

I was probably at least one beer down more than I should have been, but I took another swallow of my beer before spitting out my response.

"What are you now? Some fucking management guru?"

He smiled and ordered another drink. While we had been sitting there, he had put away three cocktails. Looked like the old man was in a mood to drink up before he went to jail.

"What are you smiling at, young man?"

I slammed down my beer.

"Nothing. Drink to your heart's content. I'm guessing some of your old pals here are covering the bill. I sure hope the Indian taxpayer isn't paying for your holiday. Tomorrow we're off and I doubt they'll be serving margaritas in prison there."

To my surprise, he began laughing, and kept laughing. Way too loudly. Loud enough that the other guests were looking at us. One of the guards looked at me, as if asking if any intervention was needed. I held up a hand to ask him to wait and shook Raza's shoulder.

"Sober up, old man. Have your drink. I'm off to my room."

As I began to get up, he grabbed my wrist, and his grip was surprisingly strong. Gone was the soft, loose flesh I had felt earlier while shaking his hand. His eyes were hard now and for a second, I got a glimpse of the ruthless killer he had been.

"Young man, I suggest you enjoy your drinks as well. With all the things I know and the kind of people I have dirt on, do you really believe they will let me stand trial? I will be bumped off in some inventive way long before people actually get to know all that I know."

I shook my hand free.

"Look, do what the hell you want. I'm off to my room."

As I began to walk away, he called after me.

"Enjoy the time you have. We are both dead men walking."

***

When I went into my room, I found Aisha and Amir asleep on the bed. She was on her back, and Amir was clutching her tight, his head on her chest, and little Georgie was lying next to him. I sat down on the sofa and just watched them for a few seconds. Whoever they were, whatever their story was, they were clearly running from someone or something, and seeing them made me remember Ma and me. Baba had passed when I was still in school and for years it had been Ma and me against the world, supporting each other, helping each other. Amir was much younger than I had been, and whatever had happened to them, he was now alone with his mother, in what looked like a pretty difficult situation.

As I saw them sleep on my bed, I decided that I might have made many bad decisions in my life but helping this mother and son duo had been the right decision. I glanced at my watch and saw that it was past nine at night. Aisha had mentioned that they would leave for their flight at eleven, and perhaps they'd want to eat something before they left. I began to get up to wake Aisha up when she moved onto her side. She had loosened a few of the buttons on the back of her dress, perhaps to make herself more comfortable before taking a nap, and I stopped at what I saw revealed. Across her back were dark, ugly welts. Criss-crossing her back. Some monster had whipped or caned her. I felt my fists clench involuntarily. What kind of monstrous man would do this to a woman? Had it been one of the men I had met at the mall? If I had known at the time, I would have killed them instead of just doing enough damage to get away. Her eyes opened and she turned to look at me. She saw where I was staring and she sat up, hastily buttoning up her dress, fumbling with the buttons and then she began to sob.

I walked up to her and sat down next to her.

"It's okay. Whoever it was, he won't hurt you again."

She looked at me, tears in her eyes, and a sad expression which I couldn't fully read.

"You can't promise that, nobody can."

Then in an instant, her old, confident face was back.

"We need to leave in a while. I'll wake Amir."

"Do you want to eat something?"

"No, we're okay."

I noticed she was no longer looking me in the eye.

She was ashamed, and I didn't want to make her any more uncomfortable than she already was, so I got off the bed and went back to the sofa. When Amir woke up, his eyes lit up when he saw me.

"Van Damme! You're still here!"

He bounded off the bed and jumped onto my lap, looking at me with his big eyes.

"We ate pizza and then we slept, but before that Mama was telling me to be careful of the bad men when we go the airport and to stay close to her. I told her Van Damme would take care of all the bad men, but she told me you weren't coming with us."

I tousled his hair.

"No, I won't be coming, but I can teach Georgie some of my moves. I'm sure he'll take care of you."

His eyes lit up.

"Really? Can you teach Georgie how to protect Mama if the bad man comes to hit her again?"

I struggled to keep my voice even as I answered I would. What kind of life had this little kid seen? I saw Aisha looking at me, her eyes downcast. When Amir went to the bathroom, I walked up to her.

"Aisha, I have no idea what you've been through, and it's none of my business, but all I can tell you is that you have nothing to be ashamed of. You're bringing up a fine boy, and you're probably taking a lot of risk to get him to a better life. That takes courage."

She broke down and began crying and when I

tentatively reached out with a hand to her shoulder, she hugged me, crying into my shoulder.

"What good is courage if I can't protect myself?"

I held her back and looked her in the eye.

"Courage isn't about always winning. It's about never giving up doing the right thing, never giving up the fight, no matter how tough things are. I don't know your story and you don't have to tell me, but I guess you're trying to get away from the man who did this to you?"

She nodded.

"I'll take both of you to the airport and if any of those men comes for you again, I swear I'll kill them. You have nothing to worry about."

Her eyes widened as she saw the expression in my eyes. Amir came out and again hugged me.

"You taught Georgie anything yet?"

"Yes, I've taught him plenty. Let's order some food for you and then we'll all leave for the airport."

I was about to call room service when I felt my phone buzzing in my pocket. It was Raza's guard.

"Some men…"

Then, nothing more.

I dialed the guard back, but there was no reply. Next, I dialed Sharma and told him, but knew that if there really was any trouble, there was no way Sharma could get to the resort in time. For that matter, his coming wouldn't do much. He was an embassy staffer here, with no weapons. He would call Sharekh, and by the time a team was organized and sent, it might be too late.

I had to go check it out.

I told Aisha to not open the door for anyone and then left to check what this new trouble looked like.

***

Raza's suite was on another floor, at the end of a long corridor. There seemed to be CCTV cameras watching the corridor, but I knew that anyone with the skills, training or motivation to come after someone like Raza would know how to deal with a few CCTV cameras. I felt totally exposed, with no weapons on me, and picked up a vase on the table in front of the elevator. I kept walking towards the suite, calling the guard's mobile and getting no response. As I got closer to the suite, I saw that the door was ajar. I took a deep breath, realizing what I'd find. The vase felt comforting to hold, but if there were men with guns still in there, then all the vase would do is ensure I died looking stupid.

I gently nudged the door open with my foot and it caught on something. I took a step in and looked around. Nobody there on the sofa, or in the small kitchenette. The bedroom door was open and there was nobody on the bed. I took another step in and saw that the door had caught on a foot. A foot that was extending out of the half-open door of the powder room. I slid open the door and saw both guards there, lying with pools of blood forming under their heads. One shot to the middle of the head. Whoever had done this had been a professional. Likely used suppressed pistols and then picked up their spent cartridge cases. That showed training and cold-bloodedness, a combination that meant trouble. I quickly scanned the suite and there was no sign of Raza.

The guards had still been warm, and the blood was still pooling under them. The call to me had been placed just a few minutes ago. If they had grabbed Raza, they wouldn't have gotten far. I had a choice to make. If these guys were breaking Raza out, they could just walk out the lobby with him. However, if they were out to do him harm, he might resist or call for help, in which case they would not go down the main elevator and through the lobby.

I thought back to Raza's comment about being bumped off and about us being dead men walking and I began to race down the fire exit as fast as I could. I knew I wasn't exactly being stealthy but couldn't afford to have these guys get away with Raza. Maybe they would torture him and put a bullet in his head, which is what he deserved, but his punishment needed to happen in India, whose people he had wronged, not in some alley in Dubai. Three floors down and I caught a glimpse of them. Two men, big, wearing suits, shoving

Raza along. I caught enough of a glimpse to see that they had taped his mouth so he couldn't call for help and his hands were taped behind his back.

I had a flower vase, up against two men with guns. Not very good odds. All I had going for me was surprise. There was no way they would know I was coming for them. As I approached them down the stairs, one of the men paused and turned around, while the other kept hustling Raza along. Perhaps he thought I was a hotel employee. Nobody else would be walking down the fire exit stairs at this time of night. He had his pistol in his right hand, which told me these guys, whoever they might me, were not messing around. They were perfectly willing to kill anyone who got in the way, and not worry too much about leaving a trail of corpses behind at a five-star resort in Dubai.

He might have got the gun up in time if I had been a hotel employee dawdling down the stairs. However, I didn't break stride and kept rushing at him, and flung the vase at him. He was good and ducked out of the way as the vase smashed into the wall behind him, shattering into pieces. I hadn't really been counting on knocking anyone out with a vase, but it gave me time to get to him before he got his gun in play. This guy might have been well trained, but his fatal error was that some part of his brain still thought I was a hotel employee sticking his nose into business he shouldn't be. He had expected me to grab the gun, or grapple with him, which most people without training would. So, he widened his stance, bringing his gun up with his right hand while bringing his left arm up across his body to ward me off.

I had no intention of grabbing his gun or grappling with him. Unlike with the bozos at the parking lot, there was no question about what I needed to do here. I needed to kill these guys as fast as possible.

I extended my right hand back, bending it at the elbow and then, with all my momentum and body weight behind it, brought it exploding out in an arc towards his face. The palm of my hand connected with the base of his nose. The nose is an interesting part of the body. Of course, you smell with it, but it also has all sorts of sensory connections with the brain. It is largely cartilage, but once you get past that cartilage, you get to bone, specifically the Ethmoid bone which separates the nasal cavity and the brain. If you smash through the cartilage with enough force and in the right direction, you can break some of the bones behind and send shards into the brain.

See, a simple soldier knows a thing or two about biology. Especially if he's taught that not to clear some boring exams but to learn how to kill people.

Sometimes works, sometimes doesn't. Most of the time, you just leave the other guy with a broken nose and in a world of pain. In this case, the guy in front of me was taken totally off guard by my strike and seemed to just stand there for a split second before crumpling to the floor. I don't know if he died because I didn't have time to check. I dove down, grabbing the pistol which was now lying on the floor next to him, and came back up in a crouch, gun aimed down the stairs, where the second man had stopped, aware now that something had just gone very wrong. He was holding Raza with his left hand, and he began to turn towards me, raising his gun.

I'm sure he was very well trained, and he looked young and fit. However, to turn around halfway, while bringing up your gun to bear on an opponent behind you takes even the best of us a second or so. The 9MM Glock I was holding had a muzzle velocity of over 1200 feet per second. Given I was only about twenty feet away from the man, the bullet I fired ate up the distance in about one-sixtieth of a second. In other words, the guy never really had a fair chance. The bullet took him in the back, near his kidney and the second bullet hit him on the neck. By that time he had almost completed his turn, he fell back, doing a grotesque pirouette and falling down the stairs. I looked down to see his body splayed at the bottom of the stairs, his neck bent at a strange angle. There might still be hope his pal had lived, but there was no doubt this one was dead.

Raza was looking up at me with wide open eyes, and I saw that he was looking not just at me, but at the gun in my hand. It was tempting. I could have shot the bastard there and then and said he had been killed in the melee. I put down the gun and took a deep breath. I had a job to do, and I'd try to do it.

"Come on, Raza. Let's get back to your room. I've called Sharma and no doubt they're coming over here with reinforcements.'

When I yanked the tape off his face, to my surprise, he didn't seem relieved. Gone was the self-assured and smug expression I had seen earlier. In its place was a look of panic.

"Don't you get it, you fool?" He hissed.

I raised the gun at his face, and he flinched.

"I thought you'd be more grateful to me for saving your sorry ass. Follow me before I blow your kneecaps out and carry you back."

He didn't budge.

"Don't you get it? Hardly anyone knew I was here. I had three plastic surgeries in the last year and was staying here under an assumed name. Just another rich businessman with bodyguards. The only ones who knew were senior folks in the Emirates and in your government and intelligence agencies. I told you they wouldn't want me to talk. I just underestimated how desperate they could be. They didn't even wait till we got back to India and it became more widely known that I had been brought back to India."

I didn't particularly care who wanted Raza dead. All I knew was that I needed to get him back to India with me in one piece, so I walked down the stairs, collected the gun from the guy I had shot and went through both their pockets. No ID, no money, nothing. Just two guns and a couple of spare magazines. The first guy was not breathing either and it seemed I had done damage to him more permanent than just a broken nose. I pocketed both guns and then pulled Raza along.

"Come on, old man. Your best chance of staying alive is with me and with the other reinforcements coming."

He shook his head violently.

"We can't stay here! I'm telling you my cover has been blown. We need to get out of here."

I had Aisha and Amir in my room and they were counting on me to get them to the airport. Raza saw me hesitate.

"Do you trust this Sharma? I ask because he's an outsider. He just came into the role a few months ago and my sources in India never talked about him being on anyone's payroll."

"Yeah, I trust him."

He grabbed my shoulder.

"Look, just get me out of here and you can call this Sharma there. I have no desire to try and make a break for it all on my own. The last few minutes have made it very clear I won't live long if I tried."

I was not going to trust a murderer and a terrorist, so I told him to fuck off. He looked hurt, but then he was not going to win too many arguments, considering I was the one holding the gun.

"Let's do this. Let's go to the lobby and wait there. Nobody will try any funny business in the lobby, and we can wait there till Sharma gets here. I have a couple of friends I need to get to the airport and maybe I'll ask Sharma for help in getting them there safely."

So, we climbed back up the stairs to the nearest bank of elevators and went down to the lobby, both guns tucked into the waist of my jeans, concealed by the coat I wore- one I had stolen from the first guy I'd killed. It was a bit big for me, but it did the job of concealing the guns, and it wasn't as if its owner needed it anymore.

***

I called my room from the lobby, and nobody answered. Perhaps understandable because there was no reason for Aisha to pick up the phone in my room. I needed to tell her that she and Amir should come down to the lobby in about half an hour and we'd leave for the airport, but I couldn't do that while babysitting Raza and while watching out for any other bad guys. So, I called Sharma to check on how far he was. When I told him what had happened, he swore loudly.

"I'll be there in fifteen minutes or so. Sharekh is bringing his guys as well, but you stay put in the lobby."

"Yeah, I have no intention of going anywhere till you get here."

I didn't tell him about Aisha and Amir because that would be a bit complicated to explain with everything going on. I resolved that I'd tell him and ask him to help get them to the airport once he reached us.

The revolving door at the lobby swung open and in walked four men. A tall, dignified looking man, with sharp features, a neatly trimmed beard and wearing an immaculately tailored suit. A businessman, perhaps. Likely a very rich businessman. The latter was reinforced by the next two men who walked in behind him. Large men, whose upper bodies indicated hours spent in a gym. Both bearded, both wearing very nice suits. Anyone whose bodyguards were as well dressed as these two gentlemen would be very rich. Raza was saying something about feeling exposed in the lobby and I was about to tell him to shut up and not whine so much when the fourth man in the group walked in.

He had a bandage around his head and was wearing a track suit.

He was one of the three men I had tangled with at the mall parking lot. Not the bald leader, but one the minions. I couldn't be sure, but it was perhaps the second minion, the one whose head I'd smashed against the car.

What was he doing here? At times I do feel like I have really shitty luck, but this was stretching bad luck too far. The businessman was speaking to the manager, showing him a photo. They were about two dozen feet away, and I couldn't see the details in the photo, but it seemed to be the photo of a woman and a child. I had a really bad feeling about this, a feeling that was confirmed when the goon with the bandage looked at me and froze.

For a second, he just stood there like an idiot, his mouth open before he began to whisper to the two large men. I got the pecking order. This guy was a thug for hire, who wouldn't dare talk to the big boss. One of the large men then approached the big boss and told him what the minion had said, at which point the big boss began to turn to look at me. Of course, I was no longer sitting there. While these guys were navigating their complicated hierarchy, I had grabbed Raza's arm and pulled him along with me through the lobby and towards the elevators. I turned to see movement behind me and knew I had been spotted.

"You're hurting my hand. What is going on?"

I had no time to answer Raza, so I just pulled him along and reached the elevator and pressed my room's floor. As the doors were closing, one of the bodyguards arrived, slightly out of breath, and put one of his paws in between the doors. I could see a handgun tucked into his waist. These guys weren't messing around.

"You need to talk boss."

The man obviously needed English lessons, but

perhaps more than that, he needed some half-decent tactical training. When someone like me is trying to run away from you and you have me cornered, you don't stop and make small talk. You get me if you can. This idiot, of course, had made the mistake of assuming I was more civil than I was and had a lower propensity for violence than I did. He stood there, gaping at me as I kicked him hard in the balls. It was almost as if he were a balloon that had suddenly been deflated, as he grabbed his crotch and bent down in agony. The second bodyguard was a few feet behind him, and I rocked back on my feet and kicked the first guy hard in the face, sending him careening into his pal. I pressed the 'door close' button frantically, hoping they'd close before the two men came at me for payback. I had two guns on me but shooting them in cold blood would be a bit of an overkill and land me in prison, so I waited. The bandaged thug was next, but seeing the two large bodyguards on the ground, and having been thrashed by me previously, he wisely decided discretion was the better part of valor and didn't move towards me as the doors closed. I knew they would know where I was headed by the floor the elevator stopped on, so I had consciously pressed the button for the eighth floor, when my room was on the seventh. Anything to buy some time.

Raza was staring at me.

"Had they come for me? What's going on?"

"It's complicated."

That was all I could say because as soon as the elevator reached the eighth floor, I dragged Raza down the fire exit stairs and ran to my room. When I opened the room, I found Aisha and Amir sitting on the sofa. Aisha, perhaps seeing the look on my face and a stranger with me, gathered Amir close to her.

I closed the door behind us and finally took a deep breath. I was having a surreal day.

"Aisha, there's a guy downstairs looking for you. Good looking, bearded, sharply dressed. He was with two bodyguards and one of the idiots we met at the mall."

She stood up, her hands at her mouth.

"How did he find me here?"

"Is he the guy…"

I didn't know how to complete the sentence I had asked, but she knew what I meant. Was this the guy who had put those marks on her? Was this the guy who had beaten her, humiliated her and caused her to try and run away with her son? She nodded.

"My husband."

I had no time to understand what the detailed story was, but I had a decision to make. Strictly speaking, whatever had happened between Aisha and her husband was their family business, and I had no right to intervene. If she had an issue with him, she should go to the cops, file for divorce or whatever else one does in such a situation. My job was to get Raza to India, and that seemed like it was no longer going to be a walk in the park, either. Continuing to try and get involved with Aisha and her son would make it even more complicated.

"Aisha, we don't have a lot of time. If he is your husband, I'm sure the police will be sympathetic when you tell them what happened to you."

She nearly spat out her reply and I could see defiance blaze in her eyes.

"The police will do nothing. He will take me away and then have me killed quietly. Nobody will even know what happened, and my son will be brought up by some other wife of his."

Raza prodded me.

"My friend, it looks like you are having a most complicated day, and it's none of my business other than the fact that it seems I depend on you to stay alive to a large extent. The men who came for me won't be the last to come for me. Once their masters know of their failure, they will send others and we are stupid to stay here."

"Shut the fuck up, please and let me think!"

Aisha glared at me, and I apologized for losing my cool and swearing in front of her kid. Amir, to his credit, grinned.

"Van Damme can swear, it's okay, mama. I've heard him swear in movies."

Aisha tugged at my other arm.

"You need to do something fast and get us out of here. If he's here, he will find out soon where we are and come for us. I would rather kill myself than go back to that bastard. He will torture me to find out what I know and then he'll kill me."

Talk about double standards. I get glared at for swearing, but she can swear in front of her kid and it's cool. I looked at Amir. He was the only one who hadn't yet expressed an opinion on what I should do. He looked at me with his big, serious eyes.

"I will not leave Mama. That man hits her and if you don't help, Georgie and I will fight him."

Well, that sealed it. I couldn't run away and leave Georgie to do my fighting for me.

Think, dammit, think! Sharma would be here soon, and Raza would be taken care of, but there was no way Sharma would get involved in a domestic dispute. He would ask me to walk away and once he told me that, I couldn't continue to get involved as far as Aisha was concerned. To do so would mean getting into some very seriously deep shit with my bosses in the government. I had been a troublemaker most of my career, and with the kind of boys I used to hang out with in Establishment 22, being a troublemaker was part of the expectations of the job, where we often did stuff the government would be happy about, but never ever publicly acknowledge or even accept having ordered. One of the lessons you learn from being such a troublemaker is the beautiful concept of plausible deniability.

I had Raza in custody. I had reason to believe there was an imminent threat and that our location was not safe. Nobody had ordered me to stay in place. If I scooted with Raza, then I could always plausibly claim that I had just acted with the kind of initiative that men like me are supposed to exercise in combat and had received no orders to the contrary. The fact that I had never asked for advice or permission would be a minor detail. Ditto for Aisha. Nobody had actually told me not to get involved. I could claim I saw a lady in distress and had reason to fear for her safety and took her along.

We'd get them to the airport, send them off to safety, and then hunker down with Raza till Sharma and company got there. Then it would all be back to normal. I would fly back to India with Raza, have no more adventures and be home with no lasting damage other than maybe hearing an earful from Rupa Aunty for not getting her baboon.

"Come on, everyone. We leave now."

I picked up Amir and asked Raza and Aisha to follow me. As we got out of the room, Aisha looked at Raza and extended her hand.

"I'm Aisha. He's helping us out."

It was an awkward moment for Raza who shook

her hand and introduced himself, saying I was helping him as well. I heard raised voices down the corridor and realized Aisha's husband and his buddies were on our floor. As we got into the elevator, I looked first at Raza and then at Aisha. Both of them had very different stories, both were trying to stay alive, and both were counting on me. Aisha knew nothing of who I was or what I did, and Raza had really no idea where and why I had picked up a woman and her son as travel companions, yet here we were.

As the elevator door opened, I saw the bandaged thug staring at me. Aisha's husband might have been very rich and clearly was a bit of a cruel bastard, but he knew nothing of tactics. He was up there with his posh bodyguards and had left the most incompetent of his men down here to guard the lifts. The man pulled out his phone and was about to dial someone, probably one of the bodyguards, when I jammed one of the pistols in his mouth. He dropped the phone, his eyes as wide as saucers.

"This gun has a silencer. I can blow your head off and nobody will even know."

He just nodded, confirming my belief that he was a low-tier thug for hire. Suppressors suppressed noise but they didn't magically eliminate all noise of a gun being discharged like in the movies. Yet, he didn't know that, so I removed the gun and then head butted him, sending him down groaning in a heap.

"Grab his phone, Raza."

Then I tucked the gun back into place and we walked out of the lobby. Raza whispered to me.

"Why did you hit him?"

Good question and I gave him an honest answer.

"These fuckers have brought the rakshas out of the bottle."

He looked at me, with some justification, as if I had lost my mind. We called a cab, got in and then we left for the airport. I closed my eyes thinking of the day I'd just had. A day when I had planned on nothing more than getting some rest, drinking some beer, and buying a bloody baboon. It had ended with four dead men, me beating up on some thugs, and picking up some pretty unusual travel companions- an underworld don whom I needed to deliver to justice and who was now being pursued by unknown killers; a beautiful woman who I honestly knew nothing about other than the fact that she was on the run from an abusive husband; her son, who seemed to think I was Van Damme, and a stuffed monkey called Georgie.

I think I'd rather be sitting in the office, filling out a Form 42.

***

EPISODE FOUR

CARS, TRAINS & PLANES

We were speeding down Sheikh Zayed Road on our way to the airport, and for a change, things had been uneventful. I glanced back at the rear seat and saw Raza looking out the right window, Aisha looking out the left window and Amir in between, playing with Georgie. I winked at the boy and then pulled out my phone to call Sharma. It was all going to be very simple. We would drop Aisha and Amir at the airport and wait there for Sharma and Sharekh to come and get us. Before I could dial, Raza tapped me on the shoulder.

"We have a problem?"

"Problem?"

He tapped me again, this time more insistently, perhaps not satisfied at my absent-minded response. I turned around, irritated, and saw that he looked very spooked.

"What's up, Raza?"

He pointed back over his shoulder with his thumb.

"We're being followed. Black SUV, two cars back."

I tried to take a look but saw a whole bunch of SUVs and more than one was black.

"Look, Raza, I don't have time or patience for games. Just sit tight and we'll get you somewhere safe soon."

I was about to turn back when he yanked at my arm.

"I know what I'm talking about! You don't lead the life I've led without developing an instinct for such things. That SUV picked us up soon after we left the hotel. I thought maybe it was another car headed for the airport and didn't pay much attention at first, but he's been maintaining more or less the same distance, slowing down when we do, speeding up when we do."

I looked over his shoulder and saw a black SUV. I tapped the driver on the shoulder.

"Slow down and move to the left lane."

A few seconds later, I saw that the SUV had mimicked our movements.

That settled it.

I looked at Raza and then at Aisha, whose face had turned pale at hearing what Raza had just said.

"Any idea which one of you they're coming for?"

Both shook their heads. Raza blurted out, "I assumed they were coming for me." and then looked at Aisha and sat back in silence. After what had just happened at the hotel, both of them were being pursued by pretty determined men. My problem was that my course of action would differ significantly depending on who was after us. If the guys in the SUV were assassins after Raza, then I'd shoot first and not take any chances. Whoever the killers at the hotel had been, taking them out or more of their buddies wouldn't get me into serious trouble. The government would bail me out since whatever I would have done would have been in pursuit of my mission of getting Raza back to India, alive and ready to face the music. However, if the SUV contained Aisha's husband and his pals, there was no way I could shoot them without landing in jail. The Emirati judicial system was known to be pretty strict, and I'm sure that shooting someone who appeared to be a pretty rich local businessman would get me in deep shit. And of course, the Indian government would totally wash its hands off me.

I groaned and slammed my hand against the glove compartment. Why did I always get stuck with decisions like this? If these were hitmen after Raza and I didn't react in time, I'd be dead. If it was Aisha's husband and I overreacted, I would probably spend my life in jail.

The driver was looking at me, terror in his eyes. I looked at his name on the license stuck in front of me. Rahil Shaikh. Either Indian or Pakistani, or perhaps Bangladeshi. Wherever he was from, he had no doubt picked up the conversation I'd just had with Raza. I took a deep breath.

"Rahil, where are you from?"

He blinked rapidly, as if thrown off balance a bit by my attempt at a normal conversation, when he had perhaps been wondering how long he had to live.

"Mymensingh in Bangladesh, Sir. Been here six years."

I took out my ID and showed it to him, then I spoke in Bengali.

"My name is Major Aaditya Sen. I'm in the Indian army and work for the government in the home ministry. I'm here on a pretty sensitive mission to get the man behind me back to India safely. There may be some men out to stop that from happening. The woman I just met today, but she's in trouble as well. She's trying to get away from a monster of a husband and I'm just trying to get her to the airport."

It felt good to just get all of that out of my system. So far, nobody other than I had known the full picture of what was going on, but I figured that if we were all going to have our lives in danger together, my unlikely band of companions deserved to know what was going on.

Then I spoke in English because I wanted my companions in the back to understand what I was saying.

"I'm sorry you're mixed up in this, Rahil, but I'll do my very best to ensure nobody gets hurt. I deal with men like these, in fact men far more dangerous than these, for a living, but not with so many non-combatants around. My first priority is to get all of you somewhere safe and then if needed, I will deal with them. Any ideas, Rahil?"

Rahil nodded violently and was about to say something when Raza tapped my shoulder.

"Major, they're making a move."

We had passed the exit to the Dubai Mall and were now headed into a stretch of the road where there were fewer buildings around. If they wanted to move in for the kill, this was as good an opportunity as any, certainly better than waiting till we got closer to the airport with more security all around. The SUV behind was now accelerating and coming to our right. Perhaps, it was just trying to overtake us.

Then I got a closer look at the bearded man in the passenger seat. He had something in his hand, something long and tubular. A barrel of a suppressed handgun? Or just a cigar? Damn. Combat was much simpler. You knew who the bad guys were, and you could shoot away. I had one of the guns out now and Rahil let out a squeak of terror, Amir cheered, and Aisha gasped.

"Easy, everyone. I just need everyone to keep their heads down and be calm. Put on your seat belts."

Then I turned to Rahil and whacked him gently on the shoulder.

"Idiot, not you. You don't put your head down and

kill us all in a car crash."

He looked at me sheepishly, terror in his eyes.

"Rahil, I told you I'm an army officer, and I'm good at what I do. Just do as I say, and I promise nobody gets hurt other than those idiots in that SUV."

He nodded as I took a deep breath and got myself ready, wondering if I was in any position to make good on such a promise.

***

The SUV was now just a car length behind, and I got a better look at the men in it. One big, bearded guy was driving, and another big, bearded guy was in the passenger seat. I wondered for a fleeting second if there was a finishing school somewhere in the Middle East which turned out big, bearded guys to act as hitmen or bodyguards. The passenger was lowering his window and I doubted it was to smoke a cigar. The object in his hand was a gun or looked close enough to a gun for me to not take any chances. I lowered my window and spoke to Rahil, keeping my voice calm and even, not wanting to panic him.

"Gently move the car to the right lane. Maintain your speed for now. When I tell you to, slow down dramatically. Don't brake hard or we'll roll over but slow down as much as you think you can safely. Got it?"

He nodded and did as I said, and I thanked my stars we had got a cabbie who could keep his cool under these circumstances. That would likely no longer hold when the bullets began flying, but I'd deal with that when the time came. The guy driving the SUV now had a choice to make. He had been planning to come up on our right where his buddy in the passenger seat would have got a clean shot at us. By moving to the right lane, I had robbed him of that. Of course, he could still cut to the right and against the traffic, but with the fast-moving traffic in Dubai, that was a dangerous move. More importantly, doing something like that would mean for sure that he was hostile. I had to know that before I did anything drastic which could get me killed or put in jail. The SUV accelerated and began to move to the right. He had made his intent very clear, and I had mere seconds to act.

"Rahil, slow down now! Raza, Aisha, heads down!"

The SUV driver was taken by surprise and his vehicle was about to slam into ours when he turned away gently, perhaps trying to maneuver and find another opportunity to get a shot at us. I had no intention of giving him another chance. I raised my gun, and I could see the passenger's eyes widen. He now had a choice to make. He could lower his gun and live or he could try and take a shot. I had my own choice to make. In the movies, at a time like this, the good guy would blow out the tires of the bad guy's car. For a fleeting second, I contemplated that. I mean, I have trained for and done all kinds of things but being in a gun battle in speeding cars on an Emirati highway was not one of them, so I had to think of whether I could even pull it off. The short answer was no. I wasn't confident in my ability to do it, wasn't sure it would even work on a vehicle moving at such a high speed and even if it did, would perhaps still give the enemy the chance to take a shot.

All of that thinking took barely a second, and in that time, my bearded opponent made his choice, and I made mine.

He raised his gun to take a shot at me and I fired thrice. One hit him in the head, and he was thrown back against the seat, his gun flying from his hand out onto the road. The two other bullets hit the windshield near the driver's side. I didn't know if I hit the driver, but that hardly mattered. With his pal's brains splattering over him and two bullets hitting the windshield in front of him, the driver lost control of the SUV and it went careening towards the left, smashing through the divider on the side of the road and then overturning in a huge cloud of dust.

"Rahil, go, go as fast as you can."

He turned to me in all earnestness, despite all that had just happened.

"But sir, if I exceed the speed limit, I will get demerit points and may be fined."

I would have laughed had we not been in so much trouble. The cops would no doubt be after us now, on top of all the other various bearded men who seemed to have decided to make my day miserable.

"Get us to the airport!"

We crossed the Dubai Creek and after a few minutes of driving, Rahil brought his car to a stop on the side of the road. I could see his hands were shaking badly.

"I can't do it, Sir. I'm a family man. I have three children back home and a wife. The cops here will beat me and lock me up."

He was sobbing now, perhaps the reality of what he'd been party to finally catching up with him. Raza pushed him in the back.

"Come on, it's just a few more minutes. Don't be a pussy!"

Rahil had treated me with politeness, even deference, but he turned and snarled at Raza, who recoiled a bit in surprise.

"Shut up, old man! I may be poor but I'm not stupid. By now the cops will have the word out and my plates will have been captured by roadside cameras. They might be coming any minute now or they might be waiting at the airport."

I motioned to Raza to back off. Rahil had a point. Even if I didn't care about what happened to him, perhaps without realizing it, he had made very good tactical sense. Anyone waiting for us at the airport would be expecting us to come in this cab. And I did care what happened to him. He was a decent man, caught up in something for no fault of his.

"Listen to me very carefully, Rahil. You go to the police and tell them I hijacked your cab at gun point and made you drive me around the city before getting off before the Dubai Creek."

He nodded uncertainty as I continued.

"I want you to promise me that you'll not mention that anyone else was with me. Just say a man hijacked you and you don't know my name."

He nodded but then I could see doubt in his eyes.

"Why would they believe me?"

Then I shot him.

He screamed and began babbling in Bengali. Aisha screamed as well, and Amir began hollering. Raza was shouting at me.

"What have you done?"

"Everyone, shut up!"

My shout got all of them to shut up, other than Rahil, who kept whimpering in pain.

"Rahil, the bullet just grazed your shoulder. They'll find the bullet lodged inside the seat. You'll bleed a bit, but trust me, there's no damage inside and you won't die or even suffer anything more than having your shoulder bandaged up for a while. Now, go to the cops and do as I say."

"What do we do?"

That was Aisha, perhaps now wondering what was going to happen to her plans of catching the flight.

I pointed left.

"We take the metro. That's the Union Metro Station and it can't take all that much time from here."

I picked up Amir as we walked as fast as we could to the metro station. Raza had seen his share of violence in his life, but he looked a bit ashen at the turn of events. Aisha was trying to put on a brave face, but I could see her hands were shaking uncontrollably. As we went up the escalator to the metro station, I held her right hand with my left.

"Hey, it'll be okay. I will get you to the airport."

She just nodded and Amir whispered in my ear.

"You're not Van Damme."

I looked at his eager face, still smiling, despite all the things he'd had to see at such a young age. The kid deserved better, much better, and I just hoped that wherever they were going, he would find a better life with his mother. He kissed me on my cheek, startling me.

"You're Iron Man."

I didn't know whether that was a good thing, since Iron Man ended up dying in battle.

***

I had never been on the metro in Dubai. For that matter, I had never been in Dubai till the day before. Raza was clearly used to a more elite lifestyle, moving about however rich underworld dons did, but thankfully Aisha knew what she was doing. She got us tickets and we went into a train where I sat down, my head in my hands.

"Are you okay?"

Aisha was sitting next to me, and I could see the concern in her eyes.

I took a deep breath before replying.

"To be honest, I know I'm not okay. I was here on a supposedly simple office trip, to get Raza and get him back to India. Look where I am now? I know I am in deep shit. All I don't know is how deep that is."

She looked down and closed her eyes briefly before she looked back up at me again, speaking in a soft, apologetic tone.

"I'm sorry. I'm part of the reason you are in the spot you're in. In fact, I'm perhaps the biggest reason. If you didn't have to get involved with me, I suppose you would have been back at the hotel right now."

That wasn't entirely true, but she knew nothing about me leaving two dead hitmen in the fire exit of the hotel. I was about to say something reassuring to her when my phone vibrated. I picked it up to see that it was Sharma.

"Sen, where are you? What are you up to? I'm at the hotel and have left dozens of messages and missed calls. Sharekh and his men are here as well, and I'm headed up to Raza's room."

Of course, I had no idea he'd been calling or sending messages. I had been too busy staying alive on the highway.

"Hi, Sharma. Things have been a bit intense."

"Where are you, Major? Sharekh just told me that Raza is also nowhere to be found, and it is a real mess here with his guards dead. What's going on?"

I looked at Raza and he shook his head frantically. When I started saying something to Sharma, Raza grabbed my hand, pleading with me to hang up.

"Sharma, I'll call you back."

I disconnected the call and looked at Raza, who seemed to be hyperventilating.

"What's wrong with you? Sharma is the one guy who could have helped us out."

Raza shook his head again.

"Don't you get it, Major? You really can't be that naïve. Only a handful of people knew that I was staying at that resort and on my way to India. One of them leaked that news or perhaps hired the men who had come for me. Those guys on the highway were professional hitmen as well, wouldn't you agree? They had two teams ready- one coming in for me in the room and one outside, either the getaway vehicle to take me wherever they wanted or another team to take me in case the first one failed."

I shut him up with a raised hand.

"Come on, someone clearly did set you up, but it

can't be Sharma. I know the guy and he's an honest officer."

Raza's eyes bored into me.

"Major, everyone is honest till they stop being honest. He's been in Dubai for a few months, right? Enough time for him to be influenced or bought over. Then there's that Sharekh. He could also be on someone's payroll."

Raza was being paranoid, but I couldn't blame him. I had learned the hard way that you never really knew whom you could trust in the world of spooks, terrorists, and killers that I had found myself in.

"Raza, who do you think would want you dead?"

He chuckled.

"That list is rather long, Major. The Pakistanis, for obvious reasons. They have the most to lose if I actually tell the Indians all I know about their terror links. Some jihadis in the gulf region won't be too happy to see me spill the beans either, because I know a lot about their networks. As I'd told you, some Indian bigwigs won't want their names in the papers after I'm done talking about all I've done for them. Finally, even the Emiratis may want me bumped off and have the blame put on terrorists. After all, I've enjoyed their hospitality and provided my services to them as well, and they won't want those details out in the open. Given they were taking me with them instead of just killing me outright, it wasn't just a kill mission. Whoever it was wanted to interrogate me first, to check what I'd already told the Indians or what other evidence I may have against them."

I listened quietly, realizing what a truly messed up situation Raza was in. I had no sympathy for the man, but now that I was stuck with him, I was in extreme danger as well. Aisha had been listening in as well and she quietly whispered.

"And I thought I had issues."

After all that I'd been through, I couldn't help laughing out loud. Amir, not understanding what we were talking about but clearly seeing the adults all worked up about something, had been quiet, also began laughing. A couple of other passengers looked sharply at us, and I finally brought myself under control.

"What the hell do we do? I am seriously out of ideas and in way over my head."

Raza leaned forward.

"For starters, going to the airport is a bad idea. We will be way too exposed."

Aisha began to protest, and he continued.

"I know you have a flight, but there are some pretty dangerous men looking for me, and now that the major has caused them so much trouble, they will be out after him as well. I'm pretty sure the airport is one place they'd cover in case we tried to make a break for it there to catch a flight out. And if the Emiratis or some Indian bigwig is involved, then they would have the cops after us as well. That's not even counting what our pal Rahil may have told the cops. He may well have told them your real name and the fact that we're headed to the airport, and we could have a whole bunch of armed police waiting for us, waiting to arrest us on charges of murder."

Now that I finally had some time to think through our options, Raza made an irritating amount of sense. I looked at Aisha and she shook her head.

"If I stay here, it's a matter of time before he gets me again. This time he will kill me."

Raza looked at her, his voice measured and reasonable.

"Ma'am, I don't know the details of your situation, but clearly your husband is not a man to take lightly. I assure you that I am a man who is used to living in hiding for years and have many connections who can help keep us safe and hidden."

I gave Raza a rap on the knuckles, and he howled in protest.

"Raza, you're not in charge. Let's get this straight before we go any further. You are a prisoner I need to deliver to justice in India. Aisha, this man is an underworld gangster who's wanted in many countries, so while he's right that many different groups of people might be after him and going to the airport has its risks, I wouldn't exactly trust him to tell us what to do."

"So, what do we do? What do I do?"

I thought it over and realized that we were now just one station away from the airport. Whatever we decided to do would have to be decided fast.

"Aisha, the men after Raza may well be waiting at the airport, but does your husband know you're taking a flight tonight?"

"No, but he could find out if he wanted to."

At that point, my phone rang again. It was Sharma.

"Major, there is such a huge shitstorm brewing here. You need to tell me where you are. Raza and you are missing, there are two guards dead in Raza's room, two more men dead in the fire exit and from what I'm hearing from the hotel management, you beat up a couple of Saudi Royal Guards. The Saudis are threatening to escalate this into a major diplomatic incident. What the hell is going on?"

I had no idea what to say so I hung up.

Aisha was looking at me eagerly, waiting for me to tell her whether we were headed for the airport.

"Raza, we're getting off here. We need to lay low for a while before we figure out what to do next."

Aisha began to protest.

"Aisha, I am in so much deep shit now that I can't go to the airport. I'll be killed or arrested. You can go ahead if you want."

I saw panic in her eyes.

"I thought I could get away, but today he's made it clear that he won't allow me to leave so easily. He sent those thugs to get me at the mall, and when that didn't work, he showed up himself with his men at the hotel. With his connections, he may well know I'm flying out and will wait for me at the airport. I don't want to go there alone. Please, I'll stay with you."

Oh, man. I had enough issues of my own without needing to watch out for her, but then I saw Amir looking at me hopefully, with his wide eyes. Why did I have to be a sucker for beautiful damsels in distress and cute kids who thought I was Iron Man?

Then I remembered something Sharma had just said.

Saudi Royal Guards?

"Okay. You know exactly who I am and what I'm involved in. I know nothing about you. If you come with us, when we get somewhere safe, you need to tell me who you and your husband really are."

***

I took another sip of the hot tea, relishing its spicy aftertaste. We were sitting in the back room of a tailoring shop, owned by an old contact of Raza's, deep inside the spice market of Dubai. When we had taken the metro from Union Station to the spice market and walked a few hundred meters into the souk, I had been stunned at this side of Dubai, so different from the gleaming skyscrapers and malls which I'd seen earlier. All around us were small shops selling spices, the colors and scents creating a heady mixture which was so unlike anything I'd seen in Dubai. The man we met in front of the store seemed surprised to see Raza but had welcomed us in warmly and told us to sit in the back room as long as we wanted. He came back with tea and told us we could sleep there if we wanted, and he'd be back with some mattresses and pillows.

My head was a bit sore. I mean, I make it sound easy, but those headbutts take their toll on me as well, and my headache wasn't caused only by that. Sure, I was trained to kill people, but killing people for the heck of it wasn't something I enjoyed. I had killed four men, men who were up to no good and would have killed me without a second thought, but as I took a deep breath and thought of each of their deaths, I said a little prayer for them, that their souls were in a better place, and if the concept of rebirth was true, then that they were reborn to make better choices than they had in this life.

"Are you praying?"

I looked up at Aisha, slightly startled. I had no idea she had been watching me.

"Yes."

"For what?"

With all I had been through that day, I wasn't up to lying about anything, so I told her. I could see surprise in her eyes and then a smile came over her face.

"You're a good man."

I exhaled deeply and sat back.

"I'm a man who is in deep trouble."

My phone rang. It was Ma.

"Ma, it's past midnight. What are you doing awake?"

"Aadi, you haven't responded to one of my messages. What are you up to? Are you coming back tomorrow?"

I had no idea when I was going back, or whether I was going back at all, but I couldn't tell Ma that.

"Things have been very busy, and perhaps I'll take a day or two more. I'll let you know tomorrow."

"You be careful, Aadi."

"Careful of what, Ma? This is a simple job."

"Nothing they send you into is simple. I know my son and I know who and what he is. They would not have sent you if it was so simple a job. Just be careful and remember what I had told you last time. Be careful of who you trust."

"Good night, Ma. Love you."

When my phone rang again, I debated whether to answer, but then I decided I had no real choice. The call was from Srini. Not only was he my boss, but he was a good man, a good officer and someone who had always trusted me.

"Good morning, Sir."

I knew something was wrong when I heard the tension in his voice. I had known him for years and while he always set high standards at work and expected the best, he had never lost his cool with me. He was one of those rare bosses who believed in inspiring his people through actions and by helping them raise their game versus crucifying them for mistakes. This was a new Srini I was hearing today.

"Sen, do you realize what you have done?"

I had no chance to say anything in reply as he continued.

"You're on the run with Raza, at least that's what the authorities there believe. They were willing to officially announce that you were helping him escape, but I held them back, saying you would have a good reason for doing what you did."

"Sir, they came for Raza and killed his guards. Those were the two men I killed in the fire exit."

He cut me off again, and I could tell that he was trying hard not to lose his cool.

"Sen, why didn't you just wait at the hotel? What made you leave? Sharma was coming there. And what the hell is this about you beating up a couple of Saudi Royal Guards? They've lodged an official complaint, and the bloody Home Minister is screaming at me for losing Raza and the External Affairs Minister is screaming at me for one of my men going and creating a diplomatic incident with the Saudis. Then on top of all that, the cops say they have CCTV footage of you shooting at a car on the highway."

"Sir, those men were trying to kill Raza."

He took a deep breath, as if trying to calm himself and spoke slowly, as if explaining something to a dull child.

"Sen, I have always trusted you and believed you. If this is what has happened, just tell Sharma or Sharekh where you are, and they will come get you. They will make sure nobody can get to you or Raza till you get on the flight."

That seemed like the logical thing to do. Of course, Srini knew nothing of Aisha, but beyond that, something Raza had said had stuck in my mind.

"Sir, how many people knew of this op to get Raza back to India?"

"Why do you ask that? Only a few people. This was a highly confidential mission."

"One of them put the killers after Raza. Till we know who that is, I don't feel confident in going to Sharma or Sharekh. I trust Sharma, but someone had to tip off the killers."

"You're being paranoid, Sen."

I gripped the phone hard.

"Sir, after what we've been through, after you nearly lost your life because someone in the IB was working for the enemy, I would have thought you would be paranoid as well. By the way, did they find out who the hitmen were?"

I think by now Srini was at least reassured that I

wasn't trying to make a break for it with Raza so he asked me to hold on and I could hear him shuffling some papers.

"Sen, the two men in the hotel were local hitmen. Hard men who had fought in all sorts of hellholes in the Middle East and would kill for money. The Emiratis say they know their past history, including some time in Syria fighting for ISIS, but have no idea how they came to be at the hotel and what they were doing coming for Raza. They were just guns for hire."

I had figured as much.

"What about the men in the SUV on the highway."

"I'm getting that info, Sen. I'll call you back in a minute."

When he did, he was back to sounding stressed.

"Sen, I didn't have to find out. The bloody Pakistanis have lodged a complaint about you killing two of their diplomats."

"Diplomats? Sir, those bastards were trying to kill us. One of them had a gun."

"Sen, I have the file open in front of me. Both were staffers at the Pakistani embassy there and the local police report mentions no gun."

Pakistani embassy staffers who'd come at Raza with a gun. Had to be ISI operatives. Srini must have known that as well. I mean, it was a pretty open secret that every embassy would likely have a spy in there- we would post an R&AW or perhaps an IB officer, the Americans would have a CIA operative, and the Pakistanis would have their local ISI guy. All masquerading as cultural attaches or something. However, what was extreme was for them to use their local ISI assets in an op the way they had. It was highly risky and something they would do only if the stakes were really high.

I suddenly felt the weight of just how badly the odds were stacked against me. Local hitmen, ISI operatives and Saudi guards. What had I got myself into?

"Sen, just let me know where you are, and I'll get Sharma and Sharekh to get you."

"Sir, I trust you more than almost any other man, but I'm asking you to trust me. We have a rotten apple in our side somewhere, otherwise so many attackers wouldn't have come for Raza all at once, the night before he was to fly out. Have you considered that maybe the local hitmen and the Pakistani ISI guys weren't even working together? That means that whoever is leaking the information has some serious contacts and money to pull all this together. Someone who can get the info out to the Pakistanis and also hire up some local hitmen. I'm willing to meet Sharma, but alone and on my terms. Please help find where the leak might be."

"I can do that, Sen, and I do trust you. Just do know that you're on foreign soil and I can't prevent the Pakistanis, Saudis and indeed the Emirati government from coming to their own conclusions about your motives. I'll try and cover for you as long as I can with the politicians."

I knew he would try his best but there were limits to what he could do. I could almost imagine the politicians frothing at the mouth when they heard of everything that had happened. They would be asking for my head, not for any conspiracy theories I might have. India and the UAE were cozying up like never before, and for me to fuck it up with all the mayhem that had occurred in the day gone by was not something they would take kindly to.

"Sir, one more thing. Why would anyone want Raza dead so badly? He mentioned he has dirt on all kinds of people, but your average Bollywood producer or industrialist won't have the balls or the resources to pull off this kind of operation."

"He's with you. Why don't you find out?"

I sincerely doubted Raza was going to tell me anything on his own. After all, whatever secrets he had in his head were the only thing keeping him alive. He would not play that card so easily.

I disconnected the call and sat back; my eyes closed for a few seconds. When I opened them, I saw Amir and Georgie in front of me.

"You look like you need a hug. Georgie is great at hugs."

That did it for me. Of all the things I'd been through during the day, those simple words did it. I gave Amir and Georgie a big hug and despite my best efforts, tears came into my eyes.

"You okay, Major?"

I looked at Raza.

"None of your business."

He smiled.

"I'm perhaps old enough to be your father, and I've now got a good sense of the kind of man you are. You are a far better man than I am for sure and unfortunately, you seem to be carrying many burdens on your shoulders. Let me know if I can help ease some of them."

"I don't think you can, old man. I'm stuck here, being chased by the police, the hitmen after you and bloody Saudi Royal Guards. My mother is old, alone and has just recovered from her second battle with cancer. I'm afraid, but not for myself. I've long accepted that in my line of work, I could die while doing my job. But if I die like this, the government won't take care of her. I'll die a criminal, someone who disobeyed orders, maybe they'll think I was helping you get away."

He was stunned into silence as I snarled out my last words.

"And you're nothing like my father. He was a soldier who died for his country, not a criminal who preyed on the weak and financed terrorists."

I turned to look at Aisha, and I could see her face had fallen. Then it struck me. I had mentioned the Saudi Royal Guards to Raza. No point hiding what I knew. After all, she hadn't exactly told me what her story was.

"I'm sorry, Major."

I tried to smile, but it was hard work.

"Just call me Aadi. The way things are going, I may not even have my rank much longer."

I had said it as an attempt at humor, but she flinched and looked down, ashamed.

"I'm so sorry to have got you mixed up in all this. I haven't said much, but I've been listening to what you've been saying about your mission and though he looks different, it's clear that this man is the infamous Danish Raza on the FBI's most wanted list, among other lists."

Danish smiled and then when he caught the expression in Aisha's eyes, he tried to look away. She hadn't meant it as a compliment.

"If it had been just you and him, you would be safe now. You could have gone to the Indian or Emirati authorities, and you'd be protected and safe. The only reason you're here is because of me. I'm sorry for that."

She had worked things out pretty clearly, and while we hadn't talked much so far, she was pretty bright to have connected the dots, and also someone who knew about what was happening in the world around her. Many people outside of India would have been unaware of who Danish Raza was.

"You have nothing to be sorry for, Aisha. Getting involved was my decision, you didn't force me to do it."

"Are you regretting it?"

I grinned.

"No. I don't regret it at all. I just wish I had the chance to teach your husband a lesson as well."

I stopped, unsure if I had overstepped and began to apologize. She stopped me.

"He is a beast, but it wasn't always like that."

Then she looked at Raza and back at me.

"For better or worse, it seems like our lives and fortunes are tied up together. I know a fair bit now about both of you and what you're trying to achieve. You know next to nothing about me. Amir is yawning and he has had a long day. Let me put him to sleep and then let me tell you my story."

***

EPISODE FIVE

GEORGIE GOES TO WAR

Raza's friend had come back with three thin mattresses, apologizing that he wasn't able to arrange anything better. We thanked him and with Amir fast asleep a few feet away, Aisha and I sat down to talk. Before we began, I gave Sharma a call.

"Major, are you going to tell me where you are?"

"Not yet, Sharma. There's obviously a leak somewhere and I want to be sure where that is before I expose Raza. We're safe for the night and I just spoke to Srini. He's trying to find out who may have compromised this mission."

"Major, Srini briefed me on the latest, but chances are he won't be any clearer on who that is for some time. What do you propose to do till then?"

Srini was trusting Sharma, and I couldn't blame him. Sharma was a good officer, and I wanted to believe he was clean, but there was no telling who else he might share the information with.

"Sharma, I was sent on a mission to get Raza back to India. I intend to complete that mission. Whoever had sent those two hitmen may send more, but for sure, the Pakistanis will be after us for the death of two ISI men. By the way, how much have you shared with Sharekh or anyone else here about what Srini told you?"

"I'm meeting him tomorrow morning."

"Tell him nothing about Srini looking for leaks. Just buy into whatever official story they will have. It'll likely be something about old enemies being after Raza. That's the most plausible explanation unless anyone wants to go looking for leaks, either at our end or among the Emiratis."

"Don't you trust Sharekh?"

"I trust nobody at the end of a day like this. I'll call you again tomorrow."

As I sat down with Aisha, I noticed Raza come over as well. Nobody had really invited Raza into the conversation, but he sat next to me. I half wanted to tell him to get lost, but the reality was that for tonight, we were stuck together. Aisha started her tale with a wistful smile, as if thinking back to more pleasant times and memories.

"My full name is Aisha Mirza. My father was of Indian origin and my mother was from an Egyptian family who had emigrated to Britain many years ago. I was born there, and life was good. We were never very rich with both my parents being schoolteachers, but I studied hard and wanted to make my parents proud. I went to Cambridge on a scholarship and then started working as a journalist with *The Guardian*."

She took out a mobile phone from her bag and tapped on it, opening a link to an article from seven years ago. Her name was there as was a photo of hers, looking not very different from how she did now. If anything, age had made her even more beautiful. She showed me a LinkedIn profile next, with a photo of hers wearing a business suit, and her qualifications listed.

"Why are you showing me all this, Aisha?"

"So that you believe me."

I began to protest by saying that I believed her, and then I shut up. I was many things and capable of many things, but in many ways, I was pretty naïve to the ways of the world. When you serve in the army in godforsaken places with only your buddies for company, life's pretty simple. You have a mission to perform, and even if that involves fighting the enemy, they are in many ways, men like you, with orders of their own. Nobody lies, double crosses, pretends to be someone they're not, or plays politics.

I nodded as Aisha continued.

"I was just out of college and had started my job. I had written a couple of online pieces about the changing role of women in the Middle East that had been noticed and I was pretty happy with how life was turning out. I met him at a conference on women's rights in London."

"Him?"

"My husband."

"Who is this guy?"

"Prince Soleiman."

That didn't ring any bells, but Raza sat up straight.

"*The* Prince Soleiman?"

Aisha looked at Raza and nodded. Raza let out a low whistle and nudged me.

"My friend, you have a knack for making bad enemies. In one day, you've taken out a couple of hitmen hired by someone big in your establishment or the Emirates, pissed off the ISI and now picked a fight with one of the most powerful men in Saudi Arabia."

When you put it that way, it did sound like I was well and truly fucked, didn't it? It's not as if I had woken up and resolved to piss off all sorts of people who would come after me with bearded thugs armed with guns, had I? I got my attention back to Aisha. I needed to know not just her story but what and who I was actually up against before they came for me again.

"I was young, idealistic, and still dreamed that fairy tales could come true. He was handsome, a prince, a real prince. He was highly educated, had been to Cambridge himself, and then served in the army. He came up to me after my speech and told me he had read and admired my articles and agreed that there was need for reform as far as the role of women in the Kingdom went. We saw each other off and on, and then one day he told me he wanted to marry me. My parents were aghast at the prospect of me going off to Saudi Arabia, but as I said, I was swept off my feet."

I saw a brief glint in her eyes as she recounted happier times, and she caught the expression on my face.

"What's the matter, Aadi? You were about to say something."

"Just that for the first time since we met, I saw you happy in thinking about those days."

"I was happy. I was delirious with joy and the first few months in Saudi were okay. I continued to write online, and while there were restrictions, such as having to cover my head, life was pretty comfortable. We'd come to Dubai almost every weekend to shop or eat, and I thought I was living a fairy tale as a prince's wife. Soleiman would be gone for days at a time, and he'd say that was part of his duty, and I didn't think much of it at the time."

"What changed and why?"

She looked at Amir, sleeping blissfully in a corner to the room, his arms wrapped around Georgie.

"When I was pregnant, things didn't change at first, though Soleiman had a lady come over and meet me to explain more about etiquette in the palace. He said she was a cousin, and I didn't think much of it. When he found out I was having a boy, he said we would need to move into the palace. Till then we had been staying in a separate villa, so that was a change. When I came to the palace, I was in for a shock. The lady who had been coming was Soleiman's first wife. She hadn't had a son and because I was pregnant with a boy, Soleiman wanted to make sure that his heir was brought up in the palace. I was told to stop publishing any more articles online and my email began to be monitored."

I didn't like where this was going. An intelligent, independent woman like Aisha being thrown into such circumstances couldn't have a happy ending.

"I confronted Soleiman, thinking he'd help me out. After all, he was the man who claimed to have loved me. He told me he did love me, but that wasn't how things worked where he came from. He had been young and impetuous but now his older brother and father had reminded him of his priorities. There had been recent trouble at the palace, his older brother was on the ascendant and many cousins and other brothers had been made to disappear. He wanted to make sure that he was in contention and had a hold on power. He tried to make it seem like he was doing it all for us. He had several wives, and he was third in line to the throne, so it was important that he have many sons to continue his line and claim to the throne after he was gone. I asked him if what I felt mattered at all, about whether all the things he'd said about women's position in society changing had been a lie or not. That's when he hit me for the first time."

I saw the haunted look in her eyes and clenched my fist. The man who hits his pregnant wife is a very special kind of asshole. If he had been in front of me, prince or not, I would have snapped his neck or strangled him with his own fancy silk tie. Aisha looked at me and I saw fear in her eyes. She had caught the expression on my face. I looked at Raza and involuntarily, he shrank back.

"What did you do after that, Aisha?"

Her tone was bitter as she responded.

"What could I do? I was trapped and whenever I raised my voice, I was beaten. He got two more wives and they were soon both pregnant, so at least I saw less of him, which was a small blessing. Amir was young and the one thing I feared most was that they would take him away from me. Soleiman may have tired of me or may have gotten blinded in his dreams of having a big role in the monarchy, but he doted on Amir, whether out of love or because as his first-born son, he was his ticket to having a stake in the monarchy in the future even if he never got a shot at it himself. The other wives gave him only daughters so he made sure I knew that Amir was going to be his heir apparent when the time came, and that if I behaved, as his mother I could also get a privileged position. Otherwise, he would just give Amir to one of his other wives to bring up. So, after a while, I tried to blend in, to do as I was told. Amir just celebrated his fifth birthday and I pleaded with Soleiman to come to Dubai to celebrate, the way we used to come in our early years together. He relented and I was out with Amir when I made my escape. Those three men you fought at the mall had been sent to get me. I have no doubt they would have beaten me badly and taken me to Soleiman."

It was now past two in the morning and Raza and Aisha both looked tired and sleepy, but something in Aisha's account didn't seem to add up entirely.

"Aisha, before you sleep, there's one thing that doesn't make sense. If Soleiman is just a father who wants his kid back, why is he bringing so much muscle and firepower along? You mentioned at the hotel that if he caught you, he would torture you to find out what you know and then kill you. What was all that about?"

Aisha looked surprised. She had perhaps said that in the heat of the moment, panicked by her husband's arrival at the hotel, hoping to get my help.

"I was pretending to be a compliant wife, to do as he wanted, but I was a journalist at heart and by training. Being in the palace meant I saw and heard a lot of things, and over time I began to gather evidence as an insurance policy which I could use if I ever needed to."

"Evidence? What kind of evidence?"

She never got around to replying because at that very moment, I heard a car screeching to a halt somewhere outside. The doors opened and slammed close and then

I heard the sound of heavy boots.

Our hideout had been blown and we were trapped with nowhere to run.

***

Aisha was looking frantic, and Raza looked out the window and closed it gingerly.

"Looks like Soleiman and three men. The same three from the hotel. Imagine escaping hitmen, intelligence agencies and rival gangs all my life, and now I die here, killed by an irate husband."

Fuck.

I turned towards Aisha.

"How the hell could he know where we were?"

She sat down next to Amir, her head in her hands.

"Aisha, who is this guy? When you said Saudi prince, I thought he'd be just a rich brat with expensive tastes. How is he tracking you down?"

She looked up at me.

"He heads up a unit in Saudi Intelligence. A unit which specializes in covert actions against people the regime considers threats."

Double fuck. This was not just an angry husband, but someone with the training, resources and ability to come after us.

"Someone like that could have bugged you or put a tracker on you. What do you have on you?"

Aisha turner her bag inside out.

"I have nothing. Just a phone, a prepaid one I bought here and the pen drive where I had the proof I had kept as insurance. That's an old one of mine from London which I'd kept hidden. I threw everything else out."

I looked at Amir, who had woken up, disturbed by all the noise in the room, and was sitting, rubbing his eyes, clutching Georgie to his chest. Raza checked the window again.

"Major, they don't know our exact location, but they know we're in the area. They're knocking on doors and are just four doors away."

I kept looking at Amir and thought of what Aisha had told me about how obsessed Soleiman was about his son.

"How long has he had that monkey?"

Amir heard me and clutched Georgie even closer to himself.

"Just over a year. I got it for him on his last birthday and he's been with it ever since. He sleeps with it and takes it everywhere."

Then she stopped and looked at me, realization dawning in her eyes.

"I don't know what your insurance policy against Soleiman is, but when you made the Dubai plan, he may have decided to create some insurance for himself."

I went and knelt in front of Amir.

"Champ, can I have a look at Georgie."

He clutched the toy even tighter to his chest.

"No. Are you going to hurt him?"

"Not at all. Remember, I had trained Georgie. Now some bad men are outside looking for us and I need Georgie's help."

I was hardly a trained intelligence operative but during my time at R&AW headquarters, I had been trained in some of the basics, and had learned through the school of hard knocks over the past year when I had crossed paths with masters in the field like rogue CIA agents and corrupt IB officers. I felt along Georgie's body, seeking anything hard or unusual under the soft, furry covering. I found something and saw that the seam along that side of the toy was a bit uneven, as if someone had taken out the original stitching and put in new ones. I picked up a knife lying in the corner and eased a few of the stitches open. Inside Georgie was a flat black disk, no than a couple of inches in diameter.

"What is it?"

I turned to Aisha to answer.

"Most likely a GPS tracker."

"Let's get rid of it."

That was the first instinct of someone who thought they were in danger. To get rid of the imminent danger. The problem was that I was not someone who was trained to just avoid danger when chances were high that danger would seek you out again. In such circumstances, I was trained to do only one thing. Destroy the threat.

"No, Aisha. They know we're in the locality and even if we throw it out the window, they are going door to door and will get us sooner or later. All of us can't escape without creating too much noise and with Amir along, we won't be able to move fast enough to have a chance."

"So, what's your plan?"

I didn't respond to Raza. If anything, he was the part of this plan that I was most uncomfortable about. The moment I left, he could easily disappear. For all he cared, he could just walk up to Soleiman and say he'd been kidnapped by me. Soleiman had nothing against Raza and would probably just let him go.

I took a look out the window. The men were two doors away and one of them had his gun out. These guys were not taking any chances this time. Soleiman was looking at his phone, his face bathed in a ghostly glow, perhaps confirming the GPS location from the tracker.

"Aisha, I'll take the toy and scoot from here. That way they'll think we're moving based on their tracker and come after me. You stay here and don't move till I get back."

Then I added, knowing that perhaps I was making promises I couldn't keep.

"In case I'm not back by daylight, assume the worst

and try and get to the airport. If that happens, just know that I'm probably dead and tried my best to help you."

Her eyes were wide with fear, but with something else.

"You would risk dying for a stranger. Why? You could apologize to Soleiman and say it was a misunderstanding and hand me over."

My eyes narrowed in anger. How did she even think I could have contemplated that? Then, I took a breath and calmed myself. She didn't know me and the world she had seen in the last few years had been a harsh one, with men like Soleiman.

"Aisha, I was a soldier, and I put my life on the line all the time for people I didn't know. Not because I'm noble or a hero, but because we all need to play our part. Some people teach kids to be better people, some people treat the sick, others make products people use. I can't do any of those things, but sometimes there are men who would harm all those who can't defend themselves and they need to be dealt with. That's a job, and someone's got to do it. Now, I have just one question for you."

"What?"

"If I have to, is it okay if I kill Soleiman?"

I could see the doubt in her eyes. I couldn't fully understand it, but then I had never walked even a meter in her shoes. The man had beaten her, had deceived her, but was the father of her child, and at one time, she had loved him. She closed her eyes and nodded and I smiled.

"I'll try not to kill him, but maybe I'll kneecap him or break a hand. The bastard deserves that much."

She looked at me and I could see her eyes boring into me.

"How can you smile at a time like this?"

"So that others don't feel as scared as I do inside."

That was the perfectly honest answer, and I don't know why I said it, but perhaps it was because I might die in the next few minutes, perhaps it was because Aisha had that effect on me of disarming me of my defenses, or perhaps because I was at the end of my tether. Aisha reached out and held my hand gingerly and then I clasped her hands in mine. She was beautiful, she was intelligent, and I reminded myself, she was married to another man and the mother of his son. We lived in two very different worlds which would never really meet. It had been an accident that had made us cross paths and soon we would part ways again, one way or the other.

I turned to Raza and grabbed his collar, hoisting him up on his toes.

"You try and run, and I promise I will hunt you down. No more caring about orders to bring you to Delhi. Do you understand that?"

He smiled and I set him down.

"Major, I am many things, but I am a man of my word. You are doing a good thing here tonight, something I can admire but perhaps never have the courage to do myself. There is a museum nearby, devoted to a famous local poet, Al Oqaili. In one of his poems called *Ask the Night,* he wrote, 'I have no supporter for my sadness except my tears.' You are providing that support and I will not betray you."

As I began to exit the back door, Amir clutched at my jeans.

"Iron Man, you'll fight all of them by yourself?"

"Ideally, I won't have to fight them, just get them away from here."

He nodded, though I could see the fear in his eyes.

"I need some help from you and your mom. Can you help me out?"

He nodded and I called Aisha over, telling her what I wanted. When I was done, I gave Amir a last hug before leaving.

"And don't worry. I won't be alone. I have Georgie along. Georgie is going to war."

***

By the way Soleiman and his men had started their search, I guessed that the tracker was accurate up to a radius of perhaps a couple of hundred meters. They had not started a broad sweep but had started looking just a few houses away. To convince Soleiman that we were on the move, I needed to get further away than that and fast. The air was cool, and there were very few lights on. All the shops had their shutters down, and unlike India, where at this time of night, you might still find a stray dog or two, everything was unnaturally quiet. I began running, starting with a flat-out sprint to put the maximum distance between me and the house and also to give Soleiman a clear sense that we were on the move. After about twenty seconds, I heard the engine of their car start up. Shit, that was fast, and I was no Usain Bolt, so I hadn't actually covered all that much distance. I sure couldn't outrun a car and wanted to put more distance between myself and the house. I spotted a bicycle attached to a house nearby with a chain. I took out a gun and shot the chain and took the bike. In the silence of the night, even the suppressed sound of the gun sounded way too loud, and I hoped I didn't have the neighbors trooping out to catch me. Thankfully, they all seemed to be fast asleep, and I took off on the bike.

It had been years since I had ridden a bicycle, and my first thought was that whichever idiot had said that once you learned to ride a bicycle you never forgot it was a liar. I wobbled this way and that and it took me a few seconds to get the hang of it. All the while, the sound of the car behind me was getting louder. Finally, deciding that a fall off a bicycle was preferable to getting shot, I sped up, pumping the pedals as hard as I could down the street. There was nobody to bump into and no traffic so I kept going as fast as I could. Soleiman must have figured we were on a vehicle of some sort with the sudden acceleration he would have seen on his screen of the tracker, and I could hear the car accelerate behind me.

I took a sharp right turn, almost falling off the bicycle, managing to stay upright by balancing against a wall with my left hand. At the speed I was going, that meant a nasty scrape on my hand, but that was fine. Better than a gunshot. You can bear almost anything as long as you think of something that would be even more painful. That's one of the things you learn being in the army and doing the kinds of things I'd done, in the places I'd done them, and the fine people I'd done them to. I kept going and heard the screech of the car as it turned behind me as I went into another alley. They still hadn't seen me, so they could be forgiven for thinking that I was with Aisha and Amir. Soleiman had no idea of who Raza was and that he was with me, and I had no doubt that he was an intelligent man, so he would have guessed I was on a bicycle, since they would not have heard any engine noises. Given he wanted Amir back so badly and wanted to get his hands on whatever evidence Aisha had, he would not come in guns blazing, for he wouldn't want to risk hitting them. Of course, when he realized I was alone, all bets were off.

Of course, I wasn't alone.

I stopped my bike near an area which I thought would be right for what I had in mind and saw that I was near a public restroom.

Why did I always seem to end up tangling with killers in the middle of the night near public restrooms? I thought back to the time I had encountered a couple of trained killers near a public restroom in the Jama Masjid area.

I abandoned the bike in the middle of the road, and then looked at Georgie.

"Buddy, this is where you need to help me out. Good luck."

I left him near the wall of the restroom, lying on his back as if he had been dropped in a hurry and then ran over to the restroom, taking cover behind one of its low outer walls. There was a streetlight on nearby which lit up the bike nicely, both so Soleiman would spot it, and so that I would have a clean shot at my targets.

The car came to a stop a dozen feet away from the bike. It was a black SUV and its license plate was interesting. It looked nothing like any other plates I had seen while in Dubai. It had some numbers but with a red border and the words 'Protocol 1' on it. I had no idea what that meant but it looked very official, perhaps even diplomatic plates. So, our pal Soleiman wasn't just looking for his wife in his capacity as an aggrieved husband. He was using official vehicles and from what Sharma had told me, Saudi Royal Guards. All that meant was that when I trashed the vehicle or killed the people in it, I would be in even deeper shit. It was too late to consider that. I had made my choice and at least Aisha and Amir were safe.

Soleiman was clearly not an idiot. The door opened and the bandaged idiot walked out towards the bike. In case there was a trap of some sort, Soleiman wanted to use his most expendable man, the hired local thug, as bait. Well, I had played these games many more times than Soleiman had so I sat tight while the idiot went to the bike, and then spotted Georgie a few feet away. He shouted loudly to Soleiman in Arabic. Given what an imbecile he seemed to be, it may have been something inane like, 'it's a toy monkey'. One of the Royal Guards was out next, hissing at the man, probably telling him to shut up. This one had his gun out, a Glock with a suppressor by the looks of it. His other pal also came out, his own gun at the ready, this time an MP5 on a shoulder sling, again with a suppressor. These guys were packing some serious firepower, and the very fact that they were ready to use them in the middle of the night told me both how desperate Soleiman was and also just how much power and influence he had.

I was outnumbered four to one. The bandaged minion didn't seem to have a gun but at the least he was a distraction to consider. If the Saudis were indeed part of the Royal Guards, they would be decently trained and moreover, they would be pissed with me. Being kicked in the balls by someone can do that to you. I didn't know how much Soleiman would get his hands dirty or whether he was any use in a firefight, but he clearly had a tactical brain, or had just learned that he was up against someone who knew what he was doing and was being cautious. I had my own set of tricks up my sleeve, and it was time to start using them.

I pressed the 'play' button on the recording app on my phone and set the volume to maximum. Aisha's anguished voice shattered the quiet of the night.

"Amir! Come back!"

Then the sounds of a muffled struggle, followed by Amir shouting out one word.

"Baba!"

Then it was all quiet again, but my recording had done its trick. Soleiman was now out of the car, a Glock in his right hand. So, the prince did not mind getting his hands dirty, after all.

"Aisha, come out and nobody has to get hurt. The man with you can go."

Too bad I hadn't recorded anything else, so there was no question of me sending out any reply. Soleiman motioned to one of his men and he crept forward, his MP5 at the ready. The bandaged idiot tagged along with him. What he hoped to achieve was beyond me, but perhaps he had his own grudge against me for beating him and his pals up.

I had a decision to make. I could start shooting and perhaps take down one or two before they began returning fire. Two issues with that. The moral and legal issue was that so far, they had not demonstrated any intent to harm me. Shooting first and perhaps killing a member of the Saudi royal family would in the best case have me extradited to Saudi Arabia where from what I gathered, they chopped off your head. I had no delusions about the Indian government risking oil and strategic relationships with the Saudi regime to save my ass. The practical issue was that I could surprise them and get one or two but then I'd be trapped in this bloody restroom. If Soleiman called in reinforcements, which I suspected he could, then I'd be dead.

Decisions, decisions. Why don't I get easy ones like whether I want extra cheese on my pizza like normal people who do normal jobs? Why do I get stuck with these crappy decisions to make?

I made my decision.

"Soleiman, I have your wife and son with me. If your men come any closer, I'll kill them."

Soleiman motioned for his men to stop and take a step back.

"What do you want with my family?"

"I want nothing to have to do with your family. I just happened to see them in trouble at the mall and intervened. When I found out who they are, and more importantly, who you are, my employer had an idea of how we could be mutually beneficial given the unique circumstances my employer finds himself in."

I could see Soleiman think that through. He had figured out by now who I was, otherwise the official complaint to the Indian government would not have been fired off so quickly. Someone of his influence would have got my details easily enough.

"Your employers, Major Sen? My people have been in touch with your employers, and they claim to have no knowledge of what you're doing."

This was where I tried to be too clever for my own good, but I had little else going for me other than the fact that Soleiman might know my biodata, but he didn't know the person behind it. He had no idea of how far I might go to achieve what I wanted, and he also had no idea of just what I was capable of, given so much of my operational record was classified.

One of my trainers had taught me that the best lies are the ones that have some connection to the truth, and I used that now.

"Soleiman, the Indian government pays my salary, but there are others who are supplementing my retirement funds."

He seemed to chuckle at that.

"Major, tell me why I should humor you? You have an army career behind you of some renown, if I go by your medals, but you're here alone, and I have three men who will take you down. I don't think you'd harm a defenseless woman and a child, so I think you're bluffing."

By way of response, I shot the bandaged idiot through the thigh. He went down, screaming and cursing. I had chosen my target carefully. Shooting one of Soleiman's Royal Guards would likely get him to react emotionally, with his ego hurt, but shooting the hired thug would have less of that impact. I also had no desire to kill the idiot, so a thigh wound would bleed and hurt like hell, but he'd be okay in a few days.

However, I had made my point. I was armed, I knew what I was doing, and I was willing to fire first and talk later.

"Soleiman, I'd say you're down to two men now, and make no mistake, I'm not someone trained to talk people to death. I used to kill people for a living. Your guards look like they're trained, and they certainly have good gear, but ask yourself, how many people have they killed? For that matter, have you ever killed anyone yourself? If not, then really think twice about messing with someone who would put a bullet through your forehead from where I am right now.'

I pressed a button on my phone and once again Amir's cry for his father rang out.

"Your son is an adorable boy, Soleiman. We don't want him to get hurt because of any misunderstanding."

The guy with the MP5 thought he was going to be a hero and he took a step forward, his gun raised to his shoulder. I put him down with two bullets to the chest.

"Soleiman, tell your men not to be idiots. I can tell from the bulge in their shirts that they are wearing vests, so this idiot won't die but his chest will hurt for a while. This is my last warning. The next time I fire, a bullet will enter someone's head."

I was sweating profusely, trying to sound as confident as I could, but I knew I was bluffing and really stretching my luck. If Soleiman knew that I was alone, he would get his men to rush me and I had no doubt I could get one of them, but against a guy with an MP5 at close quarters, I didn't fancy my chances with just a handgun.

As the Saudi guard got up, gasping for breath, and feeling around his chest, Soleiman called both his men back. The local thug was still lying on the ground, swearing in Arabic.

"Here is what I want. I represent a certain individual who is being pursued by certain elements of organized crime. We have a meeting coming up shortly where I fear we will be attacked by those enemies. I want your men to help take those enemies out."

Soleiman shouted out his response, the anger in his voice clear.

"I am a prince, and these are our Royal Guards, not your guns for hire."

I fired a bullet which cracked the windshield of the SUV, about three inches from Soleiman's left shoulder.

"And I am a man who has no issues whatsoever with killing a prince and his Royal Guards. Do as I say, and your family will be back with you."

"Fuck you!"

He must have run out of fancy, princely things to say if the best he could do was to shout abuses at me, so I shot the other guy in the chest once. He also went down, screaming and swearing.

"Soleiman, are you just plain stupid or do you want to see your son die? That idiot was also wearing a vest and will live, but you are not wearing a vest."

I saw that I had got through to him as his hand involuntarily went to his chest.

"Bad tactical thinking or maybe just plain overconfidence. Either way, things that get people killed. I want your men to put all their guns on the ground about six feet away from the wall. And also tell your two oafs to take off their vests and put them next to the guns. My gun is on your son's head."

The recording came through again for me, as I played Amir shouting 'baba', this time sharply increasing the volume, as if the boy had shouted. Soleiman motioned to his men, and they came forward, depositing the Glock and the MP5 near the wall.

"Soleiman, your piece as well. Pass it to one of your men. And if anyone has a piece hidden which they think they're being clever about, Amir's head will not resist a bullet quite as well as those bulletproof vests did."

Soleiman's face was contorted with rage, but he had no real options. As the pile of guns grew, the bandaged idiot on the ground thought he'd be a hero and tried to dive towards the nearest gun. I shot him on the other thigh, and he screamed, even louder than before.

"What kind of Indian army officer are you? You behave like a bloodthirsty animal."

That was rich coming from a man who had beat his pregnant wife, but I didn't want to bring that up, not when I was supposedly holding Aisha and Amir hostage.

"Unlike you, Soleiman, I and my brothers didn't put on a fancy uniform and get medals because our daddy was the king. We trained to kill enemies and got very good at it. Right now, you are my enemy, because you are pursuing me and have threatened me. Do as I say, and you have nothing to fear for yourself or your family."

"Okay, okay. Tell me what you want."

"First of all, I want all of you to turn around and walk to the end of the alley. Keep walking till you reach that shop with the red awning, under the streetlight. You will leave the engine running in the SUV."

"You're going to steal a diplomatic car?"

Poor Soleiman had clearly not met someone as desperate or crazy as I was. I mean, I had already shot at a bloody prince. What was stealing a car compared to that?

I wasn't in the mood for conversation, so I continued with my demands.

The men gathered together, leaving the sobbing, injured thug behind. When he recovered, I guessed he would not want to work for Soleiman again, after seeing how much concern his employer had for his safety.

"Take the idiot with you!"

I didn't care for his well-being, but I couldn't have him around, telling them that there was nobody else with me. Other than Georgie, that is.

Speaking of Georgie, I took out the tracker which I'd kept in my pockets and threw it down a nearby toilet bowl. Soleiman and his buddies began to walk back. I fired an encouraging bullet that pinged off the ground at their feet.

"Faster, your highness, faster."

As they kept going, now over two hundred meters away, almost to the point I had asked them to go to. I aimed at the nearby streetlight and fired a single shot, destroying the bulb and plunging the immediate area into utter darkness. I heard Soleiman shout something, but his men were unarmed and too far away to do much, and for all he knew, I was still dragging his family along. I grabbed the weapons, grabbed Georgie, sprinted to the SUV and began to drive away, taking a circuitous route away from the men. I was sure Soleiman was making calls to all sorts of people, asking for reinforcements, asking for more firepower, and I wanted to be as far away as possible.

I took a round and came back to the shop where the others were holed up. I banged on the door, keeping the engine running.

"It's me. Come on out!"

The door opened a fraction, and I saw Aisha's eyes through the gap, a panicked expression in them. I opened the door wide.

"Get in! Raza, where else can we hide out for a few hours?"

As they got into the car, Raza looked at all the guns on the passenger seat next to me.

"Major, what the fuck did you do? You got all these weapons and a bloody diplomatic SUV!"

I began laughing and tossed Georgie back to Amir, who grabbed him with a squeal of delight.

"It wasn't just me. Georgie helped out."

For Aisha's benefit, I added that nobody needed to be killed and Soleiman was unhurt, other than a severely damaged ego.

I saw her smile broadly and thought that she should smile more often.

"Where to, Raza? This would be a good time to think of all the underworld scum you know who would shelter us for a while and when we reach there, Aisha, you need to tell me all the dirt you have on Soleiman. I need to know what leverage I have."

As we drove away, I knew I had survived the night,

but the next day would bring even greater danger. But now I had a whole bunch of firepower, and I would have some more insider knowledge about my enemies.

And of course, I had Georgie.

***

EPISODE SIX

THE WISDOM OF KAUTILYA

Our first order of business was to dump the SUV and then find sanctuary. Dumping the SUV was simple. I knew that Soleiman would have been activating all the considerable resources he no doubt had and also getting help from the Emirati authorities. Shooting Saudi Royal Guards, threatening a Saudi prince and stealing a car with diplomatic plates was not something to take lightly, and I knew I would likely be in very deep trouble. No point in thinking about that now, as I had to focus on the immediate task at hand. I first scrubbed the vehicle to see if I could find anything useful, and did get a portable fire extinguisher, a couple of empty bottles, which I siphoned some of the fuel into, and a bit to my surprise, lots of spare magazines for the Glock and the MP5 and of all things, a flare gun. Soleiman clearly believed in traveling well-armed, and now I'd make use of these. I also found a large backpack into which I stuffed all my spoils of war and then I dumped the SUV into Dubai creek. It wasn't foolproof, as sooner or later they'd find it, but it would buy me some time. Chances were high that they would not look in the creek first, and given what I had in mind, all I needed was to buy a day's time.

In the meanwhile, Raza was trying to get his connections to help, and I was impressed. Within twenty minutes of our dumping the car, a large SUV drove up, with a very large, bald man at the wheel. He was wearing a t-shirt which seemed to be stretched almost to the point of being ripped apart by his enormous belly and seemed to never stop smiling. He and Raza greeted each other like long lost brothers, and he grabbed me in a bone-crushing hug when Raza told him that I had been keeping him alive despite some men being out to kill him.

"My name is Ali Shaikh, my friend. Raza is like an older brother to me. If you are his friend, then you are like a brother to me."

He took a look at Aisha and Amir and nodded at me.

"You have a very good-looking family. Good the boy takes after his mother and not you, huh?"

He gave a belly-shaking laugh and I decided that it would be way too complicated to explain to him who Aisha was and what she was doing with us. Besides, if he knew the kind of men who were after her, he might well reconsider how much hospitality he was going to show me or her. So, I just smiled along and then he drove us away, all the while humming the title song from a Bollywood movie.

Almost as if by way of explanation he paused his singing and looked at me.

"From India, yes? Well, I'm from Karachi, but my grandparents were from Kanpur in India. I had a small business and then moved to the Gulf to make my riches. Back then, small fry like us were always getting squeezed by the organized players. They'd threaten us, steal our consignments and occasionally rough us up. That's where Raza Bhai came in like a savior. He stood up for the small guy- all the Indian and Pakistani businessmen like me who were being threatened by the Russians and Turks. He saved my life a few times, and I, and many others here, swear by him."

Given he was in a line of business which had involved being roughed up by Russian and Turkish competitors, I thought it was a safe assumption that he didn't trade in Indian groceries or run a restaurant that served authentic tandoori food. I had long learned not to judge people, so it was really none of my business what kind of drugs he traded. For now, he was a friend, and those seemed to be in short supply. My stomach grumbled as the thought of food crossed my mind, and I realized I hadn't eaten much since the previous day's lunch.

I heard Amir giggle behind me and when I turned around to apologize, Ali slapped my shoulder.

"I will feed you the best tandoori chicken you've ever had. My own mother's recipe. Don't worry, my friend, my home is your home."

Within a few minutes, he had driven us to a sprawling house, which looked more like a fortress, with high walls and uniformed security men at the gate. We took turns showering and freshening up and then we were introduced to his family. His wife, Nadia, took Aisha in like a sister, fussing over her once she found out we were looking for shelter, and his three children whisked Amir away to play with them.

The kids were squealing in delight as they played, and Amir told him tales of how I was Iron Man and together with Georgie had beaten up a dozen bad guys. Ali's youngest, a toddler, looked at me with awe and then went back to smashing Georgie over the head. The two older kids, both girls, were perhaps not so interested in what they no doubt saw as made-up tales of adventure and fussed over feeding Amir cookies.

Given what we had been through, it almost felt surreal to be in a home like this, surrounded by the smell of cooking food and the sound of laughing children. Ali came and sat next to me.

"You were a soldier, or perhaps still are one, correct?"

I glanced at Raza and Ali laughed.

"He didn't tell me, but I've seen all sorts of people

in my life, and I noticed your hands, your eyes, the way you watch things. I know those signs. My brother is a captain in the Pakistan Army. I hope being in the home of an enemy is okay with you."

I couldn't help but smile.

"Ali, you have taken us in when we needed help. Your family has showered their love on us without even asking who we are. You are not enemies, far from it. As for your brother in the Pakistan Army, I won't lie to you, I have fought them and have both killed them and lost my buddies to them. Yet, they are not the enemy. Professional soldiers fighting for their nations have more in common than you may imagine. I may fight and kill them if I have to, and they me, but that doesn't mean I hate them. We are doing our duty to our nations, and if that means we need to fight, we do so as warriors on the field of battle. I suspect your brother and I may have more in common than we do with politicians on both sides."

He sniggered at that and then his look turned serious.

"I have a family, and I won't lie to you, I began my career doing things I am ashamed of, but I am now one of the biggest distributors of pharmaceuticals here and try to live a more or less clean life. Raza has told me a little bit of what happened, and from the weight of that bag there, I know it contains weapons."

I understood where he was going.

"No harm will come to you or your family. When the time comes, I just want your help to get Aisha and Amir to a safe neutral destination of their choice."

"You're not married?"

Ali was a good man, and he was putting his family in danger by helping us, so I didn't want to lie to him. When I told him about the situation with Aisha, he raised his eyebrows.

"You are mixed up in some dangerous business, my friend. What do you hope to gain from this?"

"Nothing, Ali, just knowing I did what was right."

"What about Raza?"

We both turned to look at Raza, who was playing with the kids in a corner.

"Ali, I won't lie to you. Raza is your friend, but he's made some really bad choices and hurt many innocent people. He needs to pay for those, and I need to take him with me to face justice."

"Raza told me that you saved him from two sets of assassins. Why didn't you just let him die?"

I looked him straight in the eye.

"I'm not the judge, jury or executioner, but my job is to take him to those who will judge him and sentence him."

He looked at me for a long time.

"You are the craziest, or the most idealistic person I've met in a long time, and perhaps there isn't much of a difference between the two. Either way, I feel sorry for the men after you, because you are also perhaps the most dangerous person I've met."

***

"What exactly is your plan, Aadi?"

Aisha was sitting on a couch facing me while Raza sat a few feet away. I hadn't exactly invited him into the conversation, but he seemed to have made himself welcome. Given how hospitable Ali and family had been, I didn't want to create a scene in front of them, and I let him sit there. The kids were now in another room, watching TV. Nadia was with them and Ali, sensing that we had some business to take care of, excused himself by saying he would attend to some calls he had with his suppliers. I told Raza to go and watch TV or something. He glared at me, but quietly went to another room, leaving me and Aisha by ourselves.

"Aisha, before I get to my plan, I need to know exactly what sort of insurance you had tried to create for yourself against Soleiman. Whatever it is, he's bringing out the big guns and I refuse to believe he's doing all that just out of fatherly love."

Aisha closed her eyes, as if bracing herself for sharing whatever secrets she had been carrying for so long, and then she told me all.

I was surprised, but I wasn't shocked, and as I heard her tale, I began to form some of the threads of my plan which hadn't been as clear so far.

I got up and called Raza back. I had not wanted him to hear whatever secrets Aisha was carrying with her, not in the least because I couldn't trust someone like Raza not to try and use those secrets later for his own gains. Given what I had just learned, I was glad that I had sent him away. He seemed to be happy to be back, part of the conversation, and since he was going to be involved in, and impacted by, whatever we discussed, it was fair that he be there, but that didn't mean I had to be any nicer to him than absolutely necessary.

"Aisha, I'm sure you've heard the saying that an enemy of my enemy is my friend."

"Didn't Churchill say that?"

"Even if he did, he didn't come up with that idea. As far as I know, that idea was expressed thousands of years earlier by an Indian thinker called Kautilya."

She looked at me strangely, as if appraising me. Perhaps she had thought all I could do was blow up things and beat up people. I could, but that's not all they taught us as Indian army officers. We were taught strategy, and I had been a good student, even if I came across as someone who tended to wing it most of the time.

"We have very few things going for us. We are outnumbered and we are outgunned, but our one advantage is that we have a number of enemies, none of whom know that the others are in play against us, or what their motives are."

"Outnumbered, outgunned and with many enemies against you being considered an advantage is a pretty optimistic view of life."

I glared at Raza, "Nobody asked for your opinion and last time I checked, you're the one who's attracting the most enemies. Keep shut or I'll be tempted to feed to you the sharks who are after you."

He shut up and kept looking at me sullenly as I continued.

"Soleiman had his trusted guards and henchmen on the job, but I doubt he'll bring the full weight of Saudi state resources. He's complained about me assaulting his men, but nothing more, and what you told me reinforces that he'll try and settle this on the quiet, because involving his brothers and father will make him look weak, and he wouldn't want that."

Aisha nodded as I continued.

"The ISI is after Raza to protect whatever secrets of theirs he has in his head, and whoever sent those hitmen has secrets of his own to protect, but if that someone is an Indian bigwig, as we suspect, then the hitmen won't be coordinating with the Pakistanis. So, we have many different enemies, who are after us, but are not working together."

"I trust you have a plan, Major."

I really wanted to slap Raza. Aisha, I had sympathy for, and wanted to help her get to safety with her son.

Raza was a criminal and terrorist who deserved whatever he had coming to him.

"Raza, I thought I told you to shut up. If you really must know, my plan is to dangle you as bait, let the sharks come and tear each other apart in trying to get a bite of you."

That shut him up, and I could see his usually self-assured, even smug look, replaced by one of increasing concern as I continued.

"That way, we not only get some of the bad guys off the table, but I also get to figure out where the leak is at our end."

"How will you figure that out sitting here?"

"Oh, I won't have to. I've got some smart friends back home whom I trust to help with that. But first, Raza, now you have some secrets to share with me. Maybe that will give me a hint about who could be the one who set the hounds on you."

Raza visibly squirmed in his seat.

"I can't just tell you all I know. I told you people would want me killed for these secrets. The very fact that I have them in my head is what makes me valuable to the Indian government. Honestly, that's probably the only reason your bosses didn't tell you to kill me and instead take me back to Delhi with you where I could try and plea for some sort of reduced sentence in return for what I know."

I grabbed his collar and shook him. I heard Aisha

take a sharp breath, but she didn't say anything more. I think by now she had understood that part of what made me tick, and kept me alive, was my willingness to back up my bark with the occasional bite.

"Listen you son of a bitch, do I look like a lawyer or a bureaucrat who will bargain with you? I don't particularly care what you know about Pakistan, Iran or any other shithole. The leak had to happen somewhere either in the Emirati government or in India. So, start talking."

He pointed with his chin at Aisha.

"Ask her to go to another room. The less she knows the safer it is for her."

That made some sense, so I asked Aisha to go and join the kids.

Then Raza began his tale and my mind boggled at just how many places he had his fingers in. Finally, I stopped him.

"Raza, this is great for the gossip columns or maybe something you can throw to the interrogators in India if they care, but I really don't think Bollywood producers, movie stars or cricket players you've paid off, influenced or supplied drugs to had anything to do with this. Let's get to the real bastards- let's talk politicians."

I was again surprised at the long list of names he had of people he had done shady deals with. What was clear was that corruption and being a general scumbag cut across party and ideological lines and reinforced my belief that politicians were bastards unless proven otherwise. He threw in a couple of senior bureaucrats whom I wasn't familiar with and then he came to some really big fish. A couple of the names made even a jaded and cynical old soldier like me raise my eyebrow, and then came a name which made me suddenly sit up and take notice.

Many of the names he had taken would have had the motive to stop Raza from testifying and taking them down with him. However, few if any of them would have the kind of access that was needed to know that Raza was being extradited to India, or indeed where he was.

It was a guess, a gamble, but it was the best card I had, and I was going to play it.

***

That evening, the kids were all asleep and Raza was sitting with Ali, reminiscing about old times over tea while Nadia and Aisha caught up in the dining room. I had been given a guest room to rest, but before I went to the room, I pulled Raza aside for a chat and leaned forward, whispering to him.

"I trust you aren't going to try and go anywhere because I don't intend to sleep."

He looked shocked and hurt.

"Major, after all we've been through together, do

you really think I'd try and run away?"

I so wanted to whack him, but that would be highly inappropriate with Ali sitting a few feet away.

"I think you're just the kind of weasel who would do that. Just remember that your best chance of staying alive is to hang with me, and if you try and run, then you'll have someone out to kill you who's far more dangerous than the men who have come for you so far. Me."

He nodded and I smiled at him.

"I remember all the dozens of people killed in the bomb blasts you financed and supposedly planned, and I would love to get an excuse to cut your throat."

He smiled ruefully.

"Major, I am not stupid. I am a survivor, and that's how I've stayed alive so many years. In the changed circumstances, where my erstwhile partners are out to kill me, I realize my best chance of staying alive is to get to India with you and strike a bargain for my life. So go and do what you need to. I'm not going anywhere."

After the events of the previous night, I could use some sleep, but I needed to get ready. I opened the bag and took out all the firearms I had collected so far- three Glocks and an MP5. I clucked in disapproval as I checked the condition of the weapons. The Royal Guards may dress in a flashy way and get high quality gear, but they didn't do so well when it came to firearms discipline. Those two jokers I had encountered wouldn't have lasted a week under the kind of trainers I'd had, who had drilled into us that guns were not a tool, they could prove to be our best friends, and like all friends, we had to take care of them. The hitmen had actually taken a bit better care of their guns, which looked to have been recently cleaned, but I thought after having been fired recently, they could also do with some cleaning. I knocked on Nadia's door and asked for some motor oil. She looked at me strangely and then handed me a bowl of oil, which I took with a rag and disassembled and cleaned all the guns. It wasn't perfect and I wished I had my gun oil and kit including brushes to clean the barrels, but it was better than nothing. I checked all the ammunition I had and realized that while the MP5 had one full clip and a spare to go with it, the Glocks between them had only two full clips given the number of shots that had been fired. I redistributed the bullets to get two full clips and inserted them into two of the guns. The third Glock had no bullets, but you never knew when an empty gun came in handy, so I kept it on the table along with the others, taking off the suppressor to ensure I knew which one it was.

Ma called and I tried to take all the tension, all the nerves I had and push them deep inside. I didn't want Ma to worry about me. I put the phone on speaker so I could continue putting aside some of the oil.

"Ma, I'm just fine. Just got caught up in some work. Did the doctor call about the check-up?"

"Aadi, I'm going tomorrow. I was hoping you'd be with me."

I gripped my phone hard. Ma was going for a scan to ensure the cancer hadn't returned and I had wanted to be there with her. Now I was stuck in a foreign land, not even sure I'd get back to Ma.

"I'm sorry, Ma. I wanted to be there with you, but I'm really stuck somewhere, and I can't return."

Ma knew me too well and I realized there was little point in my lying to her when she laughed before her next sentence.

"Aadi, I've known you long enough to know that this has stopped being just a routine office trip."

"Ma..."

"Let me finish, Major. If you are on some sort of mission that you can't tell me about, I trust that it's for a good cause and that you're helping keep people safe. Do what you need to do. Do your duty and then come home."

I felt tears come into my eyes. This was a woman whose husband had died in combat, who had seen me slip away into missions from which there was a fair chance I'd return in a flag-draped coffin, who had herself waged two battles against cancer. Yet, here she was, asking me to do my duty. When I had been younger, I had always thought that when I said I came from an army family, it referred to my father.

Now I knew better. My mother was a soldier, too. A warrior.

"I love you Ma."

I could hear her voice catch.

"Are you okay, Aadi?"

I tried to keep my voice even, but I couldn't stop some of the tears.

"Ma, I may not come back from this mission, and that's okay, because this is what I do, what I've chosen to do, and I am protecting good people, people who deserve a life of safety. But I'm afraid I won't be able to come back to you, that I won't be there for you."

I couldn't see her face, but I realized from the sniffles that Ma was also crying.

"Aadi, we are a family of soldiers. We serve in our own way, and that is what our purpose is. We serve the nation and those who need protecting. Your Baba always told me that if he didn't come back, I shouldn't cry, because knowing that I could continue being strong gave him strength when he was out there. I'll be strong, son. You be strong and do your duty."

When I hung up, I held my head in my hands and just cried for a few minutes. When I raised my head, I wiped away the tears. I heard a noise behind me and turned to see Aisha standing at the door, looking at me.

"How long have you been there?"

"About ten minutes."

I motioned for her to come in and she sat down on the sofa next to me, watching all the guns laid out on the table in front of us. She turned to look at me, an expression in her eyes I had not seen before.

"I'm sorry but I overheard some of your conversation with your mother."

"That's okay. Listen, I was about to come and talk a bit about the plan."

She shushed me and held my hands.

"You don't have to be strong for others all the time. I can see the load you are putting on yourself for us, for me. Don't do that."

"Aisha, it's my duty."

She smiled, a sad smile that never quite reached her eyes.

"Taking Raza safely to India is your duty. Not getting me or Amir to safety. Your mother sounds like a remarkable woman, and I wish I was as strong as her to bring up such a fine son all on my own, but I will try my best. Thank you for trying to give me that opportunity."

It had never been a conscious thought, but when she said the words, I realized that for years, it had been Ma and me against the world, supporting each other, consoling each other when we faced setbacks, cheering each other on. It must have been so hard on Ma to bring me up alone, and she had. I saw a glimpse of that in Aisha, the same strength, the same courage, the same desire to stand up for what she believed in and to give her son a better life. I put my hand over hers.

"Aisha, to have gone through what you have and to still take the risks you're taking tells me just how strong you are. You and Amir will get to Canada or wherever you feel safe."

"And you put yourself in so much danger on our behalf for nothing?"

I looked into her eyes.

"Not for nothing. For Amir to grow up free, for you to be free."

"Why? Why do you do all this?"

"A woman I loved told me that I should never give up on myself or others, that I needed to be the sheepdog to protect others against the wolves that are out there."

She smiled broadly now.

"She sounds like a remarkable woman. Where is she?"

Memories of Amy came flooding back and I felt a lump in my throat.

"She's dead. Those were among the last words she told me. I couldn't save her. I won't let that happen…"

Aisha leaned forward and kissed me.

I recoiled and moved back.

"This isn't right."

She was holding my hands and looking into my eyes.

"It feels right."

My mind was a total mess. She was married and I was in enough trouble as is. Yes, her husband was an abusive scumbag, but that didn't make this right. Then something came into my mind, and I hated myself for even thinking it.

"Aisha, you don't have to…I mean, I don't expect anything."

To my surprise, she laughed.

"You fool, I know I don't have to do anything, but I want to. Ever since I was a young girl, I've known only one man- Soleiman. Perhaps once he cared for me, but for years, all I've known is abuse and pain. I began to think that perhaps all men were like this, using you when they needed to, and then discarding you. You are not like that."

She leaned forward and I found myself moving forward, ignoring the voice screaming in my mind to stop, telling me this was a relationship that was doomed. We kissed and then I pulled back again.

"You don't find me attractive?"

What kind of a question was that? Perhaps she read the reaction in my eyes, and she continued, her eyes sparkling.

"Nobody has called me beautiful for years. When he was courting me, Soleiman would say it, but for years, I've had to cover myself fully, never even having a conversation with anyone other than those in the palace, and Soleiman long stopped saying anything nice to me."

"He's an idiot, Aisha. You're the most beautiful woman I've met, and what makes you beautiful is not just your appearance but the way you're trying to stand up against what almost seem to be impossible odds, to do the right thing, to do right by your son. That's what makes you truly beautiful."

She began sobbing and I held her, and we kissed again, tenderly at first and then with increasing passion.

"Aisha, we can never have a relationship. Our worlds are so different."

"We have the next hour, don't we?"

It was hard to argue with that.

Later as we lay together, her head on my chest, I couldn't help but smile. Aisha was an amazing woman, but there was no way she could be a part of my life. Best case for her was to get to Canada, apply for asylum and start a new life. With the secrets she knew and the kind of people who would be after her, the best bet for her was to change her name and live in anonymity, bringing up Amir there. With how much I had pissed off Soleiman, and the fact that the Saudis had already complained to my bosses, there was no question of me ever getting in touch with her again. If anything, my contacting her would likely put her and Amir in danger. Just my luck to get entangled with amazing women whom I was fated to not be able to be with for any meaningful period of time.

But then, as Aisha had said, did it matter how long you spent with someone? Perhaps I was fated to cross paths with remarkable women whom I could share a little while with, learn from them, make a difference to them.

But yes, with one difference. I hadn't been able to save Amy. I would make sure Aisha got to safety, even if it meant the end of the road for me.

***

To his credit, Raza said nothing when Aisha and I emerged from my room. Ali had stepped out to make arrangements for getting Aisha and Amir out of the country and Nadia was with the kids. I sat in front of Raza, and he looked at me and smiled as Aisha said she'd go and join Nadia.

"Major, since I'm the bait and I may well die, mind telling me what exactly you have in mind?"

Perhaps because of the time spent with Aisha, I was in a mellow mood, or perhaps we were getting closer to the endgame with a very real possibility of Raza or me, or both of us, not staying alive to see the next morning. Either way, I smiled at him.

"Sure, why not?"

He seemed surprised by my response, and he smiled back as I began.

"Kautilya again. He had said that there were four strategies to get anyone to do what you wanted them to. Saam, daam, dand, bhed."

Raza beamed now, like the kid in class who's got the answer.

"I remember that. Not that I read anything in any

classroom like you, but there was an old TV serial. But how does all that apply to our case?"

"Let's start with the easy one. Saam means offering advice or asking someone nicely. With Soleiman we're well beyond that stage, and with the kind of men out to kill you, I don't think asking them to please not kill you would have much of an impact."

Raza roared with laughter, and just to ensure he didn't mistake my better mood for my going soft on him in any way or suddenly considering him a pal, I threw in the next line.

"Though your life is one of the bargaining chips I'm putting on the table as part of Daam, which means offering incentives or a quid pro quo."

That shut him up quickly.

"For Soleiman, I'll obviously offer up Aisha and Amir in return for his doing his part and the goons after you will be coming because they want you."

"How the hell will you get word out to the ISI and whoever hired those hitmen?"

"I won't need to Raza, because of Bhed- which means using secrets against your enemy. I think I have a hunch on who might be the one orchestrating the attempts to kill you from the Indian side. Even if I'm wrong, I'll shake the tree and something or rather someone will fall out."

I could see concern writ large on Raza's face.

"You will stake my life on a hunch you have?"

"Well, to be honest, I have more than one hunch on who may be behind this, and I'll try and cover all the angles. Hopefully someone will bite."

"That's very reassuring."

"Don't try and be sarcastic. If you've got a better idea, I'm all ears."

He just looked sullen but said nothing as I continued.

"When it comes to Soleiman, I am much better placed when it comes to knowing some secrets he would kill for, literally. I will use them."

"What secrets and how will you use them?"

I smiled at Raza.

"I could tell you but then I'd have to kill you."

He began to smile and then the smile disappeared as he looked at my eyes and saw that I wasn't kidding.

"You seem pretty confident for a man who's up against three sets of enemies."

I held his gaze.

"If I were to be totally objective and logical, our chances of success are less than fifty percent."

His eyes widened and he thought I'd follow that up with something. When nothing else was forthcoming, he exclaimed, his voice high-pitched in surprise.

"You're joking, right?"

I just held his gaze, and he knew from my expression that there was no humor in my words.

"We are totally screwed then, Major, if you yourself

feel your plan has less than fifty percent chances of success."

Then I finally smiled.

"Raza, soldiers don't work on logic. If a soldier's actions were dictated by logic, he'd get a job sitting in an office somewhere. It's inherently illogical to risk your life over a piece of land you've never been to or to shoot another man who has done nothing to personally offend you, and whom you don't know at all. So, soldiers don't give a rat's ass about logic and that's the edge we have."

Raza was looking at me intently, as if seeing something in me he had not seen before.

"We get things done because we believe in our mission, and I believe that Aisha and Amir should get a better life, and once a soldier believes in a mission, he will do illogical things for it."

"What will you do?"

"Kautilya's last stratagem- dand. Punishment. Violence. If nothing else works, if I can find no other way out to achieve my mission, these men have no idea whatsoever how violent I can be. I will kill every single one of the fuckers I can before they get me. I can't fight and win against all of them, and quite probably they will kill me, but they have no idea what's in store for them if I stop playing around and start killing."

As I got up to make a call, Raza sat there, stunned into silence.

***

"Sen, you do realize just how much pain I'm feeling right now. Short of the Prime Minister himself, everyone has called me and asked me why one of my officers is killing Pakistani diplomats, causing mayhem in hotels in Dubai and pissing off some Saudi officials."

I could tell from the strain in his voice that Srini wasn't having a particularly good day, and so I just let him rant for a while, to get it out of his system. To his credit, he never blamed me. That's the hallmark of a boss you'd do illogical things for- someone who trusts you even when everybody else is saying the opposite.

"Sir, I really appreciate your sticking your neck out for me. I really mean that."

He chuckled.

"Sen, spare me the sentimentality and tell me what you want. As promised, I've been shaking some trees and unfortunately, if we go back far enough, almost everyone from film stars, Bollywood producers, cricketers, industrialists to politicians has had something to do with Raza."

That was consistent with what Raza had told me, and with what the gossip columns had been hinting at for years. No journalist had of course dared to take names, because the one or two who had tried quickly found themselves out of jobs, threatened or roughed up.

"Sir, it has to be someone senior in the political establishment. Only someone like that could line up the ISI and get hits ordered in the gulf."

"Sen, I can't walk up to ministers and ask them if they were in bed with Raza and want him dead before he testifies against them. I'll lose my job."

My voice was dead serious when I answered.

"Sir, these people won't end at getting you fired. More likely you'll die in an accident."

There was silence on the other end for a few seconds.

"What do you suggest, Sen?"

"Sir, don't take it on yourself. Say that the PM has asked you to do discreet background checks on some senior ministers to ensure that they had no links with Raza before Raza gets there because he wants to make sure that all information on Raza is kept strictly compartmentalized before the trial. Tell them that this is because we've had a couple of attacks on Raza here and that I am lying low with Raza and will come in only when we're sure that there is no leak at our end. Firewall all information by saying Unit 22 has been given special jurisdiction based on a request from the PMO. It's close enough to the truth."

I could almost hear Srini cough up the coffee he was probably drinking.

"Have you lost your mind, Sen? I can't just take the PM's name like this."

"Yes, Sir, you can. You report straight into the PMO through the big boss, and you have been independently leading this, so it's plausible that you could get confidential requests like this from the PMO. You can say that you brought it to them because you didn't want it to be awkward for them if they later found out about it and that being someone who is loyal to them, you wanted to let them know discreetly. Imagine how the PM would feel about a PR nightmare blowing up in his face about someone in his party being in bed with Raza? Far from being pissed with you, they'll be pleased. Then you can tell them where I'm bringing Raza in and how. I still need to work specifics on that and will let you know."

Srini chuckled aloud.

"You are learning how to be a bureaucrat and an office dweller, Sen."

"God forbid, I'm just reapplying what you taught me. Isn't this pretty much how we caught Ravindran in the Intelligence Bureau when we wanted to confirm whether he was in bed with the enemy? You're the one who told me how to go about that, and this isn't a very different plan. If they're clean, they'll deal with this through official channels, maybe even complain to the PM. But if one of them is our guy, you're virtually dangling an irresistible bait to the people behind this. If they see that they have a shot at getting Raza and me at the same time, they'll come in swinging."

"Sen, how does that help? They'll come in at you, and I won't be able to do much sitting in Delhi. If this were in India, maybe I could rustle up the Unit 22 boys you'd worked with last time, but I can't get them to

Dubai. Should we at least alert the Emiratis?"

"No, Sir. I have no idea who in the Emirati security establishment is compromised. But here are a couple of people you should definitely pass on this message to."

I think Srini coughed up the rest of his coffee at those names.

"Do you have any proof whatsoever, Sen? Telling people like those that Raza has dirt on them will get them to explode."

"Sir, to be honest, I have no proof, but only a couple of people in the current establishment would have the motive, opportunity, access and influence to pull off the kind of attacks we've faced. Both names are being talked of as being potential PM candidates in the future, so stakes are high for them, and Raza named both of them as people he's done dirty work for in the past. He's maintaining his own insurance policy and tells me all the documents he has are in a Swiss bank locker, but on this, I believe him. He has no reason to lie since he knows it's his life on the line. Don't put this through any of the other normal official channels. Go straight to both these men and say that you came to them directly because of the sensitivity of the information involved and because you wanted to be discreet. If they're clean, they will bounce this up normal channels or ask you to investigate. If one of them is dirty, he will deal with it himself and we'll know who he is."

Srini took a deep breath.

"Assume I do all this, and the bad guys come at you in force, what's your plan to stay alive and get out of there in one piece?"

"I'm working on that, Sir, but just a heads up. Be ready to have the Saudis complain a bit more."

"Why?"

"Because some of them are going to get involved in a pretty nasty war without knowing why, and because there's an outside chance a prince may end up getting killed."

He said nothing to that. Perhaps there was nothing to be said to something like that. Then he took another deep breath.

"Sen, you could use a few friends. Sharma is clean. I've had all his records, bank statements, and calls checked. There's nothing to indicate he has anything to do with any of the men after you. Bring him in and he can help. If nothing else, it shows that you were on official assignment working with me as part of Unit 22 versus totally going rogue, which is what currently things look like."

I hung up before I looked back. Raza was staring at me, his eyes wide with disbelief.

"You are a crazy motherfucker. Do you realize what you're going to do?"

I went into the room and gathered all the guns and came out, lugging the bag on my shoulder.

"I didn't start this war, my friend. All I wanted to

do was come to Dubai, stroll about for a day, and then go back to India with a gangster and a baboon. I would have been happy to walk away, but now it's too late for that. They started the war, and the only way we can get back to India alive is for us to finish it. Ready, Raza?"

"Ready for what?"

I could see fear in his eyes, as if dreading what I was going to say.

"Ready to go to war?"

***

EPISODE SEVEN

RUSSIAN ROULETTE

"Major, I trust you know what you are doing, but this is ridiculous."

Sharma was trying to be professional, but his face was turning red, and matters weren't helped by Amir laughing loudly and pointing out to Georgie that the new uncle was very weird.

"Sharma, I am offering up some bait, so I need to have something concrete to show."

He took a deep breath and sat down, muttering about looking ridiculous in the burqa he was trying on. To be fair, that hadn't been my idea, but Raza's. I knew about combat and war, but the old man had spent his life among devious men, and obviously had ideas I might not have naturally thought of.

An hour ago, I had called Sharma and asked him to come over to Ali's place, but to make sure he came alone and didn't tell anyone else about it. I knew from bitter past experience how much spies loved to bug phones, so I had actually given him the wrong address, some five houses down, and laid in wait for him, armed with two Glocks. If he turned out to be playing for the other side and brought other bad guys with him, then I'd drop them and think of a new plan. Thankfully, Sharma seemed to be as clean as Srini said he was, because he showed up, all alone and looking pretty clueless when I had walked up to him and tapped him on the shoulder. It had taken twenty minutes to bring him totally up to speed on everything that had gone down. He thought my plan was crazy, but then he had no credible alternative to offer given the circumstances. If our operation was compromised from the inside, then there was no way we were going to be able to pretend things were normal and try and take Raza back to India the way we had originally planned. He didn't seem too happy about the added complication of Aisha and Amir being in the picture, along with Soleiman and his thugs, but I made it clear that getting them to safety was now part of the mission, or I wouldn't play and I would just kill all the Royal Guards who came my way, get them on a flight to Canada, and Sharma could figure out all by himself how to get Raza back alive, or stay alive himself for that matter. He hadn't enjoyed that conversation, but what he was enjoying even less was my plan of taking him along, wearing a burqa.

"Sharma, it's not a bad idea Raza has come up with.

I know you feel ridiculous, but you're roughly the same size as Aisha."

He looked up at me.

"What does Srini Sir say?"

Sharma was a good man, but he was a career bureaucrat who wanted to make sure the boss knew and was aligned to what he was going to do. I, on the other hand, was a combat soldier. In my line of work, you of course got your objectives and mission parameters cleared with the boss, but then you improvised and did what was needed to get the job done. In combat you couldn't afford to pause every few minutes and get permission from the boss, and frankly, in the line of work I had been in, sometimes it was better for all concerned if what we did and how we did it was known to very few people.

"Srini will be okay with what we do, as long as we get back alive and get Raza back with us."

"Do you think the ISI will fall for this?"

That I was sure of. I had killed two ISI officers. No matter what the ISI bosses feared about Raza's revelations, their men in the Emirates would be after my blood, driven by sheer vendetta if nothing else. I got it. I would have done the same thing if someone had killed a couple of my buddies as well. I had nothing in particular against the men who would come for us. They were professionals doing their job, most likely with no idea that their bosses had made their fortunes on drug-running and passing guns and money to terrorists in cahoots with Raza and were sending them to kill and be killed so that their misdeeds wouldn't come out into the open. However, they would try and kill me, and I would try and kill them back. That's the story of soldiers in every conflict in every country in the world- you fight and kill men whom you perhaps have nothing much against, often because your masters are using you to build their empires or drive their agendas.

What I wasn't sure about was the number, nature and capabilities of the hitmen who would come for us. But that was something I couldn't control, and it wouldn't help to worry about it.

We sat down for dinner, which ended up being a slightly surreal affair. The kids of course had no idea of what was going on and shouted and joked and horsed around the way kids do. Georgie seemed to be a huge hit with Ali's kids, and he got a place of his own, and Amir pretended he ate up all the dessert so there would be none left for us. Nadia knew that her husband's visitors were not just friends out on a tourist jaunt and seemed a bit on edge. Ali himself knew that we were reaching the end of our road, and perhaps all he was hoping for was that whatever happened, his family be spared any danger. Raza sat quietly through dinner, looking glum. I could understand why. The last couple of days had been chaotic and stressful, but he had been free. Two days ago, he had nothing to look forward to other than sitting in an Indian jail and in a worst case, hanging from a rope in some time. I wondered if some part of his mind was contemplating whether dying would be better than sitting in a jail for years. Aisha was sitting next to me, and throughout dinner, she held my left hand with her right, gripping it tight, knowing that it was quite possible that we would never see each other again. Sharma was just giving me dirty looks, now that I had laid out my plan which included him going out to meet a Saudi prince dressed as his estranged wife.

After dinner, Sharma pulled me aside again. Raza was with us, as was Aisha. She wasn't going to come along with us, but she knew that her ability to get away to safety with Amir depended to a large extent on how things unfolded over the next day.

"Major, you always seem to be confident. I'm shitting bricks here."

I had to grin at Sharma's honesty.

"You are being way too hard on yourself, Sharma. I've seen you with a revolver taking on four terrorists armed with AK-47s."

Something changed in Sharma, and he seemed to stand just a bit taller, his shoulders just a bit straighter.

"It's okay to be scared. I'm scared as well, but the only way we can get through the next day is to keep going in spite of that fear. To take that fear and turn it into anger. Anger at the men who think they can kill us and get away with it. Got that, Sharma? Some men are out there who want to mess up your job, mess up your life, perhaps kill you if you happen to come in their way. And you know what should piss you off even more than all that? The fact that they think they can get away with it and we can't do anything to stop them."

I turned to Raza.

"How are you doing?"

I think I surprised him, because for a change I hadn't snapped at him, or told him to shut up. I may have hated his guts and wanted him to hang or rot in jail, but in the day ahead, he was a comrade, who would need to watch my back, just as I would need to watch his.

"I'm okay, I guess. When I was younger, I would take risks and get into dangerous situations, but perhaps I was never as crazy as you are."

We all laughed. That was a good sign. When you know you're headed into danger and a lot of things are going to be outside your control, you need to be able to keep your heads, and a big part of that is being able to keep a sense of humor. Getting high-strung leads to mistakes, and mistakes get you killed.

"Aisha, you and Amir will fly out by tomorrow afternoon. Ali is arranging it."

She didn't say anything in front of the others. After a few minutes, Raza retired for the night, sharing the study room which Ali had converted into a makeshift guest room with a double mattress.

"Sharma, you take my room. I'll stay with the scoundrel."

Sharma had grinned at me, and it was good to see his spirit returning.

"Major, you've had enough adventures in the last couple of days. Let me babysit him and you get some sleep. I suspect our walking away alive will depend a lot on you, so we all need you to be rested and on top of your game."

"Anything more from Srini?"

He winked at me.

"He's calling me in an hour with the latest. I'll tell you in the morning."

"No, I'll be up. Just come over and tell me what he says."

As I went to my room, Amir came up to me and hugged my leg.

"Iron Man, Mama says that we are leaving tomorrow. Come with us."

I knelt in front of the boy.

"Champ, I can't do that. I have to get back to my own Mama, but you don't need to worry about a thing. I've taught Georgie all I know, and he's actually fought some bad guys with me. Just watch out for your Mama, will you?"

He saluted.

"Yes, Sir!"

I ruffled his hair and sent him on his way to the

kids' room when I heard footsteps behind me.

It was Aisha.

She motioned to me to go into my room and as soon as we were inside, she kissed me.

"Aadi, I can't leave without even knowing what happens here. Without knowing what happens to you."

"You have to. The best window for you to get away is when Soleiman and his men are being kept busy. Even if he has local cops on his side, they will also be racing to reach the scene of where we will be. Ali's already got his contacts lined up and is confident he can get you on a flight to Canada tomorrow afternoon. Go there and ask for asylum. With your background and British citizenship, you should get asylum there. In a worst case, hint at some of the stuff you could help them or US Intelligence with, but ideally don't get mixed up…"

I couldn't finish because she kissed me again and held me tight. When she looked back up at me, I could see tears forming in her eyes.

"I wish we had met somewhere else. I wish we had different lives."

The same thought had crossed my mind, but I knew that wishing for things that could never happen was not a particularly good line of thinking to pursue. I sat down on the bed, and she sat next to me.

"Aisha, maybe how we've met, where we've met is all meant to be."

She smiled and I felt myself wishing I could see that

smile every day.

"I didn't know you were a philosophical or religious type."

"I'm not religious in the sense of going to temples very often or following rituals, but when you've been in the line of work I've been for so long, you tend to believe that things happen for a reason, that good men die because there is some meaning in that death, that even when bad things happen, there is something good to look forward to, that if you do what's right, you will succeed, maybe not now, but eventually. It's either that or you believe that the world is a giant clusterfuck over which you have no control."

She laughed, and I was glad she did. I didn't want my last memories of her being ones tinged with sadness.

"We have just one night left."

"Yes."

She moved closer to me and bought her face close to mine.

"Then let's not waste any more time."

***

I heard the knock on the door and quickly dressed and went to it, knowing Sharma must have got the call from Srini. Aisha was still asleep, and I turned to look at her, thinking that this might well be the last time ever that I saw her. My plan was to leave early in the morning to scope out the location where I had tentatively planned to lure Soleiman and our other pursuers. When I opened the door, Sharma looked excited.

"Major, looks like someone's taken the bait."

We went back into the living room and Sharma called Srini again, this time putting his mobile's speaker on at a low volume.

"Sir, Sen here."

"Looks like your plan worked, but I'm afraid it may have worked too well."

"What does that mean?"

"One of the men you mentioned went ballistic. He literally went red in the face saying he had nothing to do with the likes of Raza. Then he said we should take this to the Prime Minister because he wanted to defend his honor."

"So, you think he's clean?"

Srini chuckled.

"Hardly. You know what Shakespeare wrote about the lady doth protest too much."

Actually, I had no clue. I had read what was required to pass English back in school, but since then, I had no time for Shakespeare, but when Srini was in one of these moods, it was best to keep quiet and let him continue.

"I checked on some of his money matters. Seems he was mentioned in the Panama papers, something that he managed to hush up by paying a bunch of money to his media contacts. So, he's a corrupt bastard all right, and he may well have had some links with Raza in the past. After all, which of our current politicians has not? But I suspect that may have been linked to getting drugs or women, not nasty business which he'd be in bed with the ISI for. I gave him an hour to cool down, but he was serious about calling the PM. I checked with the PMO, and he actually took an appointment to go meet him. I had to then catch him and tell him that he didn't need to do anything, because some Secretary in the PMO had made the list and the PM had personally said that we shouldn't check on him given his clean image and proven loyalty."

"He bought that?"

Srini gave an exasperated sigh.

"Sen, I don't know. I hate working like this. Making stuff up as I go along. I would normally have planned this out much longer. I can only hope he has bought the story, otherwise if he does go to the PM, then we are all screwed."

When Srini swore then he was in a really bad mood. Any other boss would have chewed me out or fired me, but Srini was not that kind of boss, for he could see what was of value after sifting through all the chaos and fog of war.

"With the other one, Sen, seems like we've hit jackpot. He was totally quiet, said nothing when I laid out what we had agreed. He simply told me that he understood that I needed to do my duty. I cannot tap the phone of someone like him without authorization, but we do tap and intercept communications of all sorts of people they might call at a time like this. The ISI guy at the Pakistani consulate here got seventeen calls today from a landline which I know belongs to the mistress of this gentleman, and our IB friends told us that some underworld handlers we track had their phones buzzing all day, getting calls from the same number. These are the kind of guys whom we know are involved in organizing hits or big operations working together with the Pakistanis. We don't know who they will send but clearly our man is reaching out to all his contacts.'

"Who is it, Sir?"

"Sen, this is a secure and encrypted line, but I won't take names. Suffice to say it's a man you once pissed off a lot."

I felt a sense of calm come over me. It was one thing to fight against an unseen and unknown enemy. When the enemy got a face and a name, he was just another man, and all men can be killed.

"When we're done here, Sir, I want a shot at him."

I could almost hear Srini sputter in disbelief.

"You'll do no such thing, Sen. You get Raza here and I'll make sure I get straight to the PMO with this, and we'll burn the bastard, but we'll do that through proper channels. As is, you're in deep trouble, with all sorts of complaints coming in. If you manage to pull things off tomorrow and get Raza here, then at least we can make those go away. I mean the Pakistanis will wash their hands off the whole thing and claim they had nothing to do with the attacks on Raza and you, and the hitmen who might be sent will anyways not be mourned by anyone. I do hope you know what you're doing because you're up against some pretty tall odds. But there's one piece of trouble which we'll need to work harder on solving."

"We'll be fine, Sir. What's that trouble you mention?"

"The Saudis. They're screaming at us, saying you assaulted their Royal Guards and stole a car."

No mention of Soleiman. He was trying to lean on me without putting himself in the picture. That wasn't unexpected but what came next was a bolt from the blue.

"Sen, they're also saying something about you helping a fugitive princess escape. I hope those are just figments of someone's imagination. The government will back you up on everything else because those are all linked to your mission, but we can't protect you if you're getting involved in Saudi internal matters. Please tell me that's all hogwash."

"It is, Sir. She's not a Saudi princess."

I swear I heard a loud noise as if Srini had dropped and broken something.

"What are you saying, Sen?"

I hung up. Bad career move, but what else was I supposed to do? Sharma was looking at me with a tight smile on his face.

"Always the troublemaker, Major."

"Does that bother you?"

His smile broadened into a grin.

"No, that's what has kept so many of us alive."

We sat down on the sofa. It was almost two in the morning, but I doubted I'd get any more sleep. Judging by how high-strung Sharma seemed, I guessed it was the same with him.

"Major, what's bothering you?"

'The Pakistanis will now bring out their top game. I guess some of their bosses would want the dirty laundry Raza has on them to never be displayed, plus their ops boys will want payback for me killing two of them. I doubt they'd have enough boys to do their dirty work in Dubai itself, but it won't be a huge issue for them to fly in some reinforcements for their cultural attaché."

Sharma grinned. We both knew that the resident spies were often holders of innocuous titles like cultural attaché.

"What I don't know is what kind of firepower the underworld may send against us. They're doing it only for the money, and the kind of enemy we are up against has no shortage of money. I just wish we knew what kind of opposition we were up against. Would also help us play Soleiman accordingly."

"Russians."

I spun around, seeing Ali standing just a few feet behind me. For a man of his size, he had moved like a ghost. Raza was standing at the doorway to the room where he and Sharma had been sleeping, just behind Ali.

Ali sat down beside me, while Raza kept standing.

"My friend, I've been hearing news from my contacts over the last few hours that the Russians are pulling together an all-star team for a big hit. I couldn't help but overhear your conversation and if it helps in planning, then you need to know that it's likely the Russians who will be coming for you."

I just looked at Ali, who met my gaze and didn't flinch. He had said he had put his past behind him and was now a pharma distributor. How a law-abiding pharmaceutical distributor knew about movements and plans of the Russian mob was something I didn't want to ask him. He had been nothing short of a lifesaver for us, and I wouldn't insult him by asking him how he knew what he did. Instead, I asked him something that was of more concern for me.

"Ali, won't you and your family be at risk if you get involved at all in finding out information and later word gets out that you helped us? I had promised you that nothing would happen to you or your family."

He clapped me on my shoulder, his bear-like paws jarring my bones.

"My friend, that's why I respect you so much. You would rather put yourself in harm's way than bring harm onto a total stranger and his family. That shows honor, and that is very rare in today's world. While you were sleeping, Raza filled me in on the details of what you are involved in, and I must say you have balls of steel and values that most people would say are old-fashioned, if not outright suicidal, in today's day and age."

I began to protest but he hushed me with a raised arm.

"Values which I admire, my friend. Raza is an old pal, someone I owe big time, and I would not have let him go into harm's way without helping if I could but now that I know what you are mixed up in and the fearful odds you are up against, I can't in good conscience let you handle those enemies all alone. My family will be fine. My business partners find my services invaluable, and I have some powerful clients and customers whom I can call upon for help if I need to."

"Who are these Russians likely to be? How good will they be?"

I had pictured big, fat, blond hitmen with bad accents of the sort James Bond movies had ingrained in my head. I had done all kinds of dirty work with and against all kinds of special operators, terrorists, and insurgents, but the world of organized crime was alien to me. What Raza said didn't do much to increase my confidence in our chances of survival, let alone success.

"These boys will almost certainly be ex-Spetsnaz. Russian special forces. Well trained and with good gear. Usually, they operate in pairs but knowing who you are they may send more."

Sharma and Raza must have seen the changed expression on my face on hearing the news.

"Anything wrong, Major?"

I didn't answer Sharma at first, running through scenarios in my head. There were few which ended with me being alive.

I asked everyone to sit down and asked Ali if he had anything to drink. He came back with a glass of orange juice.

"Anything I could mix that with?"

He raised an eyebrow, perhaps unsure of what I was saying but Raza caught on and whispered into his friend's ear. Ali came back with glasses and a bottle of Absolut vodka. As I poured drinks for everyone, Ali took his sheepishly.

"I don't drink, you know."

"I know, a mild-mannered pharma distributor like you wouldn't be mixed up in any bad habits, would you?"

I had said it with a wide grin, to let him know that I meant no offence, and he grinned back, taking the glass. I drained my glass and poured another before I began.

"Well, boys. This is now getting to be serious

business. In the army, we'd get rations of alcohol, and we'd drink up before a particularly tough deployment, to enjoy each other's company and talk shit, not knowing if all of us would be back together again."

I could see from their expressions that they were all worried now.

"Those local hitmen were little more than street thugs with suits and guns. Soleiman's Royal Guards have never actually seen combat and spend their time accompanying princes to fancy locations and eating in five-star buffets. Spetsnaz boys will be a whole different level altogether, as good as any of the men I've served with. I could take one of them, perhaps, if it was my day, but I can't take three or four of them."

I could see Raza on the verge of panic. He'd been counting on me to keep him alive and now seeing my confidence shake was making his face turn pink.

"Ali, what relationship do the Russian boys have with Al-Qaeda?"

I could see Ali start to protest that he wouldn't know such things but then all three of us glared at him. Now was not the time for him to pretend he had nothing to do with the murky details of the underworld in the Middle East.

"They hate their guts. Many of their senior officers had fought in Afghanistan, Chechnya and some of the newer Russian boys fought in Syria. So, they hate Islamists. I've met some of these Russian boys and while they're all now, shall we say, privately employed, they are still fiercely patriotic."

I had an idea coming into my mind, taking a plan whose chances were already razor thin into the area of the highly wishful, but then I had few options.

"Ali, I need to talk to the Russians."

His eyes went even wider than they had been.

"Major, these are dangerous men who have been paid to kill you."

"Well, tell them I have something for them that is worth more to them than the money they may have been promised. Tell them I want to meet someone senior, someone who had served in the early 2000s in the Russian forces. In the meanwhile, I need to talk to Aisha to fill in some gaps in what she told me and do a little bit of research."

Sharma grabbed my hand.

"Are you sure about this?"

"No. But when life gives you a lemon, what do you do?"

He hesitatingly offered his answer.

"Make lemonade?"

"Not just lemonade. You pour some vodka in it and drink up."

***

The man in front of me was bald, stood a good four

inches taller than me and was built like a tank, with his biceps bulging over his huge chest as he crossed his arms in front of him, looking at me with his piercing blue eyes. He was pretty intimidating in and of himself, but for good measure he had two of his men, who looked to have been created out of the same mold, though slightly scaled down versions of their boss. It was five in the morning and as soon as Ali had made his calls, I had been summoned to an abandoned warehouse near the desert.

"I am Captain Konstantin Vasilyev. You are a brave man or a mad man. You know we are paid to kill you and the man you protect, and you ask to meet us. I was told you would be a hard man to kill which is why I was here personally along with two of my best men. Yet, here you are, all alone, unarmed, asking to meet me."

"I'm Major Aaditya Sen. Our paths have crossed in strange circumstances but like you, I served my nation, in the Indian army's Paras and then in the SFF. We trained several times with your boys. They were very good, and their vodka better."

Vasilyev's expression softened a bit.

"I even learned some Russian from them."

Now he was genuinely interested and leaned forward a bit.

"Do dna!"

That was Russian for bottoms up, a phrase repeated often when the Russians and our boys would gather after exercises over drinks.

"And I could sing one of Oleg Kukhta's songs, but believe me, you don't want to hear me sing."

Vasilyev roared with laughter and the men behind me chuckled. His arms came down by his side, on the table between us.

"I actually knew Oleg. Better soldier than he is a singer, but that's just my opinion."

Oleg Kukhta was a former Russian special forces officer who had gone on to become a very successful musician. He had served in many combat zones including Chechnya.

"Captain, I wanted to meet you because I thought we could talk things over and then let you decide whether you want to proceed with the assignment you've been given or choose an alternate course of action."

Vasilyev looked over my shoulder at the two men behind me.

"Why should I not just ask my boys to kill you, collect our money and go home?"

"I was a soldier once, captain, like you. I would like to believe there's more honor among us soldiers than that."

"What do you want me to do then?"

"I won't insult you by telling you what to do, but someone like you may want to value honor over money."

He leaned forward, his eyes boring into me.

"Speak in plain English, boy. What honor are you talking about?"

"Beslan. Very nasty business. Chechen terrorists taking over a school, over 300 people killed including many kids."

The veins in Vasilyev's neck seemed to be bulging and he gripped the table hard as his voice became a dangerous whisper.

"I was there. I carried out dead kids with my own hands and blew out the brains of some of those animals who massacred the kids. Why do you speak to me of that horror?"

"Because I can give you the man who arranged the funding for it, in return for letting me and my man go."

His eyes were now narrowed, and I knew I was looking at a ruthless killer, one who wouldn't hesitate to kill me if he thought I was trying to pull a fast one on him.

"You have proof?"

"Abu Omar Al-Saif."

Vasilyev visibly stiffened at the name.

"The Saudi cleric and terrorist who was among those who funded and organized the Beslan massacre. He was killed in Dagestan in 2005, I think."

"What of that camel fucker?"

"I know the man who funded him. The man whose money was behind Beslan."

Vasilyev's eyes had taken on a feral look, of a predator on the hunt.

"I imagine it's some Saudi bigwig. We know the fucker got money from Saudis through a network of charities. Those were wound down and the Saudis of course claimed they knew nothing of all that nasty business."

I leaned forward now, trying to play my trump card at the right time, when I knew enough to be confident that the Russians would bite. Ali had told me what he knew about the background of some of the Russians who were involved in the assassination for hire business in this part of the world, and if Vasilyev was the top honcho of his crew, then it was a fair bet that he had the same employer Ali had mentioned.

"How long have you been here in the Middle East, captain? Men like you don't just kill for money paid by fat politicians and underworld dons. I imagine that's a side business of yours. What's your real job?"

Vasilyev hesitated and then I leaned forward even closer.

"The Wagner Group is a good paymaster from what I'd heard, and your bosses work directly for the Kremlin. I imagine they would look really good to the Kremlin if you took out the man behind Beslan."

The Wagner Group was a firm which hired out Russian private military contractors, typically former Special Forces soldiers like Vasilyev. Officially, it was a private firm and used its men to provide security duties, but in reality, it was used as a proxy army by the

Kremlin in places like Syria, putting trained Russian killers in places where the Russian army couldn't go without creating a major diplomatic incident.

"You know a lot for a retired soldier who's babysitting some fugitive."

I grinned, happy to hold some of the cards.

"I'll level with you, captain. I'm not a retired soldier. I'm a serving officer in the Indian Research & Analysis Wing. I work in a special force called Unit 22. I used to be on the frontlines, doing the messy stuff, but now I sit in an office, supposedly doing a desk job, but as you can see, I still seem to get stuck with the messy work."

I could see that Vasilyev was surprised, and I gently took out my ID and put it on the table in front of him.

"If you want, my boss can call your boss and clarify matters. The man who's hired you to kill me is in fact someone my bosses will take down for collaborating with the enemy. I am not here just as a loose cannon or a man whom you've been paid to kill. I'm here representing the Indian government."

That was seriously stretching the truth because, other than Srini and Sharma, not a single Indian officer knew I was here. I imagine if the PM or the other senior brass learned I was making deals with Russian hitmen on behalf of the Indian government, they would throw a fit. But what they didn't know couldn't hurt them. More to the point, it was my neck on the line and if I wanted to have a ghost of a chance of emerging alive, getting Raza back and helping Aisha and Amir escape, I had to play all the cards I had, and bluff my way through, pretending I had a few I didn't actually have.

He studied my ID, and then spent more time studying my face, as if deciding whether I was telling the truth or bluffing. He seemed to relax and sit back, apparently satisfied that I was being truthful.

"This is more complicated than I thought. I was told I was to kill an underworld figure with a trained bodyguard. That's all."

"Of course, the man who arranged this hit would never have told you that you were supposed to kill a serving Indian officer. I doubt you'd take such an assignment up because it would really complicate your life with your bosses back in Moscow if they ever found out such a thing or if my bosses complained about their mission being disrupted by Russians."

He nodded, and then his eyes narrowed.

"This man, the one who supposedly funded Beslan, must be someone big in Saudi Arabia. I suppose your bosses know that you are offering him up to me."

I couldn't help laughing at that.

"Captain, I suppose you keep your bosses fully updated on your side business, including who you killed and how much you earned?"

He roared with laughter, and I could hear the two men behind me laugh as well.

"This can be our little secret. You don't have to tell

your bosses you got any of the info from me. Say you got it from some Islamist you caught or something."

"My bosses will need proof that I have identified someone like this."

I took out my phone and called Aisha.

"Aadi, thank God you're okay. I've literally been praying all morning that you would be fine."

"I'm okay. Don't worry about me. Can you send over a couple of images of the file we had talked about?"

When the images had come through, I showed Vasilyev my phone.

"Receipts and letters of thanks from Benevolence International to the man I can give you. Benevolence International was a Saudi charity which was banned in 2002 after it emerged that it was one of the top financiers of Al-Qaeda and its boss went to jail. The man I offer to you helped channel Saudi money to Benevolence International. Check the next photo."

Vasilyev's grip on my phone stiffened as he saw the image.

"Yeah, that is what it looks like. An Arabic letter with the English translation handwritten below it. The letter is from Abu Omar Al-Saif, sent to this man just after the Beslan attack in 2004. It praises Allah for guiding the hands of the martyrs and thanks this man for his help."

Vasilyev looked at me, murder in his eyes.

"Who is this Soleiman mentioned in these documents?"

"At the time he was a very young man, driven to Islamist ideology by his teachers and wanted to join the jihad against the West by going to Afghanistan and joining Osama Bin Laden in his fight against the Americans there. I have evidence that he went there to meet Osama and transferred money to him and enabled some weapons transfers to Al-Qaeda, but that's something the Americans might be more interested in than you. His parents forbade his actually getting into the fighting, so he began to use some of the considerable money he had at his disposal given his role as a senior official in the government to fund Benevolence International and others like it to fund jihadi attacks. His family found out about it, but decided to keep quiet, either because of the scandal that would erupt, or perhaps they actually approved of the cause. Who knows?"

"He would have to be a very rich and influential man to be involved in all this."

"He is. Years later, once he saw that he could be set up for real power and his past connections with terrorists and murderers would be inconvenient, he tried to put it all behind him. Luckily, one of my friends has a bunch of evidence on his connections and many of the attacks he helped fund."

"Who is he, Major?"

"He is a prince in the Saudi Royal Family. Third or fourth in line for the throne if I'm not mistaken."

At that Vasilyev's eyes widened and he let loose some abuses in Russian.

"You come to me with all this and then tell me the man is someone I cannot touch. How will I and my boys ever get to someone like him, sitting in Saudi, with all his guards and army? Even if my bosses get to know this, it will be delicate to say the least. It's not as if they can call up the Saudis and ask them to hand over a prince. Our government and the Saudis are all playing nice now, for weapons sales and oil. I don't think they would ever openly confront the Saudis about something like this."

"I understand, Captain. Politicians the world over are the same. They won't ever confront the Saudis openly, but if the prince is taken out somewhere else, in a way where the blame can be plausibly put on someone else, or even on an accident, your bosses won't be displeased with you and the initiative you took. More than that, I imagine you'd enjoy getting some personal payback for what this sick fuck helped happen in Beslan."

Vasilyev's hands gripped the table hard.

"I would wring the bastard's neck and cut out his eyes if I could get a shot at him, but how is that possible?"

"He's here, Captain, and if you choose to deal with me, I can arrange for him to be at a place where you can get him. Kill him or capture him and take him to your bosses, that's your choice."

Vasilyev grinned broadly.

"You are a resourceful man, Major."

"No, I'm just a man trying to complete a mission and get home."

"I can understand that. All soldiers can."

He nodded to the men behind me, and I heard them put away their guns in their shoulder holsters.

"Captain, I should warn you. This is not just a fat Saudi prince. He has some training, and he travels with bodyguards with bulletproof vests and decent gear. When he shows up, he may well bring reinforcements which I can't fully predict."

"We can prepare for that. Boris, call the boys and say we need a few more here with some heavy gear."

Then Vasilyev turned back to me.

"What makes you so sure this prince will come when you call him? What does he have to do with you?"

"He wants to kill me."

Vasilyev laughed, tilting his head back.

"You are a popular man, aren't you? Well, why does he want to kill you? How can a man like you be mixed up with a man like him?"

"I'm helping his wife run away."

He stared at me for a full couple of seconds and then laughed even more loudly.

"Stefan, get the good stuff."

Both of his men pulled up chairs around the table and put down a bottle of Zyr vodka and four glasses.

Vasilyev poured into each glass and then nudged one towards me.

"I think we will have a busy day ahead of us, Major. Let us part as friends over a drink together."

I raised my glass and emptied it.

"Do dna!"

***

EPISODE EIGHT

DUST TO DUST

"Hatta". When I had laid out what I had in mind, that had been Ali's one word answer. Any soldier knows that terrain plays a major role in determining whether you win or lose, and in this case, I knew next to nothing of the local lay of the land, and gratefully accepted Ali's suggestion. Before Sharma, Raza and I left, I got a few minutes with Aisha and Amir. Amir hugged me tight, perhaps realizing that this was it. The final goodbye. When he let go, I could see that he had tears in his eyes.

"Amir, you're a big boy now. I need you to be brave and strong so that your Mama and you can find a new home."

"Will I never see you again?"

"Never is a big word, champ, but yeah, for some time I think it'll be best if we don't look each other up. You'll be just fine. I've seen how brave you've been through all these days."

"I was scared all the time."

"So was I. I still am, champ."

His eyes widened.

"How can you be scared? You're Iron Man?"

I chuckled at his childish enthusiasm. I prayed it stayed that way as long as possible, without getting crushed by the harsh reality of the world we lived in.

"I'll settle for just being a decent man. Being scared is okay, as long as it doesn't stop you from doing what's right and helping others. Will you remember that?"

He nodded his head vigorously, and then held out his precious stuffed monkey.

"You take Georgie."

"I can't do that. He's your best friend."

He held our Georgie towards me, pushing the toy into my chest.

"I want you to have something to remember me by."

I kissed Amir on the forehead and then looked up at Aisha who nodded.

"Take it, Aadi. We won't exactly be posting Facebook or Insta photos of our time together, so it'll be nice if you have something to remember us by."

I grinned and followed Aisha into my room, where she hugged me tight.

"Will you be okay?"

"I'll be fine. I'm more bothered about you. Will you be fine?"

She looked up at me and kissed me.

"Don't worry about me. I'll be just fine. Whenever you miss me, hold Georgie close."

I smiled and kissed her back and then gathered the bag with the guns. Waiting outside for me was Sharma, looking pretty miserable in his burqa, and Raza, who looked only marginally less pissed off.

"Remind me, Major, why don't I get to carry a weapon?"

"Because you're a criminal who's in my custody. Clear?"

Raza looked glum but said nothing more. Sharma had arranged a rental car and he drove, with Raza beside him in the front and me in the back. Hatta Heritage Village was a replica of an ancient village some two hours drive away from Dubai, and the photos I'd seen on the net reinforced my belief that Ali had chosen well. There was a fort, complete with a citadel and ramparts, which would offer unparalleled views and line of fire all around, and a bunch of low-lying shops and buildings. It had been closed for renovations, and everything about it looked tacky and literally shouted out that it was a tourist trap. That was okay with me. I had no intention of doing any sightseeing and I had a very different sort of trap in mind.

On the way, I started making my calls. I wanted to make sure that we got there first, and that our various friends didn't get too much of a heads up to put too many new variables into play.

The first call was to Srini.

"Sir, let our friend know that I'm bringing Raza in at the Hatta Heritage Village where Sharma will meet me and together we will go to the airport. Please wait thirty minutes before letting him know and tell him that we'll be there by two thirty in the afternoon."

"Will do, Sen. I'm actually getting you three tickets on a flight that gets out at eight at night, so all going well, you should be back home tonight. With the kind of mayhem you may create, it may be good for Sharma to get back for some time till things blow over. Tell him I've covered his bosses and they agree. I've also smoothened things out as much as possible with the Emiratis, so they shouldn't give you much grief. Now just get home in one piece."

"Thank you, Sir."

The next call was to Soleiman, whose number I had got from Aisha. I wanted him and his men to be there first. If everyone joined the party at the same time, we were toast, because I wouldn't have the time to make any of my plans fall into place.

"Prince, I'm on my way to Hatta with my man. I expect that his partners will try and double cross him and attack us there, so I need your men to help out."

"So, Major. I checked up on you since we had some time after our last meeting. It is strange that someone of your background and with the impressive track record you had chooses to work for some shady underworld don for money."

"Medals don't pay the bills, Soleiman. Now are you in or not?"

"What about my wife and son?"

"Your wife and son will be with me, and soon as you do what I'm asking you to do, they're all yours. We walk away and never see each other again. Be there at just after two in the afternoon."

"I would hope for your sake that we not cross paths again."

Well, that wasn't being too friendly. Next up were the Russians. Vasilyev growled into the phone.

'Do you have him?'

"I will, Captain. I am texting you some photos, so you know what he looks like."

He sniggered.

"No need, Major. The FSB has been giving us a lot of information about this man."

That was fast work, and impressive. The fact that Vasilyev had not just managed to get his men together for this mission, but also got clearance from Moscow and got the Russian Intelligence Service to help, told me that he was much more than a freelancer working for a private military contractor company.

"Captain, because we shared drinks together and because you are helping, you should know that other than Soleiman, there may be other bad guys there who may come in the way. Just call ahead to let me know what vehicles you're coming in, so I don't mistake you for bogeys. Be there by two in the afternoon but don't come to the fort. Wait somewhere where you have a clear line of sight of the gate. You'll know my signal to attack when you see it- a single flare. Just remember, there may be bogeys beyond Soleiman's men."

He chuckled.

"You are a real troublemaker, Major, are you not? Don't worry, I am coming with quite sufficient resources to take care of business."

Sharma looked back at me briefly.

"You sound like you're inviting people for a party."

"Sharma, it is going to be a real blast of a party."

***

When we approached Hatta, I had to admit I was impressed. From the descriptions I had heard and the few photos I had seen on the internet, I had expected tacky construction and over the top props to wow gullible tourists. I should have known better. As I had remarked about the Emiratis earlier, they built things big, and they built them fancy. There was a bloody honest to goodness real fort, complete with high walls with ramparts encircling the village. The village itself had a gate blocking our entrance and Sharma stopped the car and looked back at me for instruction.

"Drive through the gate, man."

He gave a long, exasperated sigh. Knowing Sharma, I imagine it was less about the act of breaking the barrier and more about the paperwork he'd have to do to file an expense claim to convince government accountants that the damages to his rental car were justifiable in the line of duty. We crashed through the gate and were soon inside what turned out to be a dusty, grey mishmash of low huts and buildings. There were a few discreet signs for toilets, ticket registers and shops, but those had been tastefully engraved into the baked earth and stone buildings.

As we got out of the car, I took a long look around and smiled. This was even better than I had imagined as a place to host our little party. There was only one entrance, and the high walls gave both excellent cover with the ramparts and also great line of sight to observe whoever was coming our way. I had a fair amount of firepower, though I was hoping Soleiman and the Russians would provide most of the fireworks. All I was missing was a pair of binoculars. I spotted a souvenir shop to my left and turned to Raza.

"Break that window and go in and get a couple of pairs of binoculars."

He looked at me for a second before answering.

"That's breaking the law."

"Fuck off, Raza. Don't tell me you've never broken any laws. I suspect stealing a couple of binoculars here wouldn't even make the list of your infractions."

He gave a sheepish grin as I waved him on.

"If it helps with your conscience, drop in a hundred-dollar bill."

He did as I asked, and came back with two binoculars, still looking glum.

"Cheer up, Raza. If anyone here has the highest chance of dying, it's me. You and Sharma are wearing the two vests we had."

"Yeah, but you have all the guns."

It was impossible to argue with the man, so I just ignored him and climbed up to the top of the ramparts and looked out over the surrounding desert. No sign of anyone yet. It was hard to predict when the different guests would show up. The most unpredictable of the lot were the Pakistanis, and the most dangerous. The Russians were at least nominally on my side, though when the bullets started flying, I wouldn't be counting on that to stay alive. Soleiman wanted his son and his secrets safe, so he wouldn't come in guns blazing without being sure he was getting what he wanted. The Pakistanis on the other hand were coming in for a pure kill job- to get rid of Raza to please their bosses and to get rid of me to take revenge for their fallen buddies. I saw a message on my phone from Vasilyev, saying that he was coming with his men in two white SUVs and that they were no more than fifteen minutes out. I asked both Raza and Sharma to scan the desert in all directions for any sign of approaching vehicles and then I called Soleiman.

"Where are you, prince?"

"We're coming in. I can see the fort. We're in three black SUVs."

Raza tapped my shoulder. He had spotted Soleiman's convoy. I quickly gave him and Sharma their instructions and then we got ready.

"Prince, I want you to stop in front of the gate."

The three vehicles came to a stop and no less than ten men got out with Soleiman. All of them were wearing vests and carrying MP5s in their hands with Glocks on holsters at the waist. Soleiman himself was wearing a vest and had a handgun in his right hand. He looked up, glaring at me.

"So, we finally meet face to face."

"As I promised, your family is safe and sound."

I motioned with the gun in my hand to my right and Sharma got up, covered totally in the black burqa, peering over the rampart. He was literally shaking, and for a moment I thought of telling him not to overdo the acting, and then realized the poor man was shaking with fear and nervousness. It was unscripted, but it worked. Soleiman chuckled.

"Aisha, my darling. No point being afraid now. It's a bit late for that."

With that, he raised his hand and fired a single shot into Sharma's chest. Sharma spun around and fell heavily to the ground with a groan.

"Soleiman, are you out of your mind?"

He grinned up at me- a feral grin. Gone was the sophisticated prince. Now he was the man whom Aisha had seen, a cruel man driven by his own insecurities and dark past.

"I have no need for the bitch. I just need to make sure she's dead, and once we're through here, I'll put a bullet in her head. I do want my son. Tell me what you want of me, and I and my men will do it and take my son."

I just looked at the man. To be honest, till this point, I had been in two minds about whether I should kill Soleiman or let Vasilyev's men kill him or capture him. The only reason that thought had even crossed my mind was because I didn't want Aisha to think of me as a monster who had killed the father of her son. Now that I saw the kind of man he was, I knew that I didn't give a damn if he ended the day with a bullet between the eyes or if the Russians took him away to string him up by his balls.

"What are you smiling at, Major?"

"I'll give the signal for Amir to be brought out. But before that, you do need to do something for me."

I took out the flare gun I had appropriated from Soleiman's car and fired a single flare into the sky. Some of Soleiman's men looked up at the flare, tracking its path in the sky over their heads. Bloody idiots. They should have been watching me.

Well, that's the first rule of combat.

The dumb die first.

Soleiman looked at the flare and then up at me.

"What do you want me to do?"

I now held up both hands, a Glock in each.

"Die."

I began firing, moving from left to right. Putting a shot with the right handgun into one target, followed by a shot from the left hand one. One to put a man down, the second to ensure he stayed down. All the men were wearing vests and I couldn't be sure I'd kill or even seriously wound them, but I had total surprise on my side. When my guns clicked empty, I saw that six men were down. Most had taken shots to the torso and were just stunned, but at least two were bleeding from wounds to the legs or arms. Soleiman had done many dirty things, and perhaps sitting in his comfortable office or home, he had imagined himself a mujahideen, taking vicarious pleasure in jihadis he funded to kill infidels. However, he had clearly never been in real combat. When I had been firing away at his men, instead of shooting at me or doing anything that remotely approached taking charge of the situation, he had decided to hide behind the open door of his SUV.

I dropped both handguns and picked up the MP5. Two Saudi guards were now returning fire, pretty much a waste of time and ammunition when your target is hiding behind the ramparts of a fort. I shouted out to Sharma to check if he was okay. He had taken the covering off his face and head and nodded, though his face was flushed. Raza was to my left, crouched low, watching through a gap in the ramparts.

Where the hell were the Russians?

I had been counting on them joining the party. If it was going to be just me versus some eight or nine pissed off Saudis who could still stand and fire weapons, then I was going to have a very exciting, and very short afternoon at Hatta.

I heard shouting in Arabic, and realized Soleiman was reasserting control over the situation, telling his men to stop shooting, or at any rate, to stop wasting their ammunition. When the idiots stopped firing, he shouted out to me.

"Have you lost your mind, Major? What do you hope to achieve by firing at us? Give me my son!"

By way of answer, I pointed the MP5 over the rampart, moving it in an arc and squeezed off a whole magazine on full auto. The clip holds thirty rounds, and the MP5 on full auto can fire at close to 800 rounds a minute. Do the math. In a couple of seconds, thirty rounds had sped towards the Saudis. I hadn't aimed, and wasn't trying to hit a particular target, but a couple of shouts told me that some bullets had hit home. I was just trying to keep Soleiman and his gang occupied while Vasilyev got into the act.

Where the fuck were the Russians?

As if by way of reply, I heard Raza shout.

"What is that?"

This I had to see. I peered through the rampart and saw a smoke trail emerge from behind a nearby sand dune.

"What is that? Slow for a rocket, isn't it?"

This time it was Sharma.

The smoke trail closed on the Saudis. I knew what it was. It was a rocket fired from an RPG shoulder held launcher. Sharma was right. An RPG rocket was considerably slower than a bullet, in fact a rocket fired from a typical Russian RPG launcher starts off at a speed of just over 300 feet per second and then accelerates to less than 1000 feet per second. If that sounds fast, consider that it is well under half the speed of a bullet fired by an AK-47. That's why you can see an RPG snaking in on you, trailing its telltale smoke. Of course, you'd be an idiot to keep watching it come towards you.

The Saudis heard Raza and began to turn, but it was all too little, too late. The rocket hit the last vehicle and I heard a distinct pop, followed a split second later by a huge explosion, which turned the vehicle on its head, showering the men nearby with shrapnel. I knew what had just happened. The first pop had been the first smaller warhead designed to create a hole in any armor, and the second warhead was the larger charge behind it, designed to go through the hole made by the first and explode inside.

The mad fucking Russians had brought armor-piercing RPGs with them.

Now, this was going to be a real party.

Raza stared at me in incomprehension as I began laughing.

***

Soleiman was screaming something, but his men were beyond caring. At least five lay dead or critically wounded on the ground, not in any position to bother about what their boss was saying. The other men were up and about, but too terrified at the prospect of rockets flying in at them to listen to Soleiman, who was now screaming in English. Too bad for them because he was actually making some sense. He was asking them to get into the village, because sitting behind the SUVs would hardly protect them from rockets. One more RPG snaked in and exploded next to another SUV, taking down another Saudi. That got them to pay more attention to their boss and they began to retreat inside the village when two white SUVs came roaring in.

One masked man was leaning out of the front passenger side in each SUV, firing away with Kalashnikovs. At least the Saudis had the sense to use suppressors. The Russians were truly mad. Blasting away with RPGs and Kalashnikovs on full automatic in the UAE was a recipe for trouble, unless they knew that and had their own connections to smooth over things with the Emiratis. One more Saudi fell before the others gathered inside the village, hidden behind a large well. The Russians fanned out and took positions, and I could see a masked figure, considerably larger than the other men, shouting orders in Russian. That would have to be Vasilyev.

After a few more bursts from the Russian rifles, an uneasy calm descended upon the village. There were just four men left with Soleiman, and the Russians outnumbered him by a wide margin, with nine men including Vasilyev. However, Soleiman and his men were behind good cover and Vasilyev was a smart soldier and didn't want to lose men needlessly. I didn't see an RPG launcher with the Russians and could only guess that they had run out of rockets. He shouted out to Soleiman, trying to bring an end to the proceedings.

"Give yourself up, Soleiman, and your men can live."

"I don't give a fuck about my men. I'm not giving myself up."

I shook my head. I mean, Soleiman must have paid his men insane amounts of money to put their lives on the line for a scumbag like him. Sharma, now over the shock of having been shot and nearly killed, crawled over to me and nudged me.

"Could you kill Soleiman from here?"

He had a point. The Russians were just below

and to the left of us and Soleiman and his men were crouched to the right. They were no more than thirty meters away, and while Soleiman was concealed from the Russians, I could see his head and most of his shoulders. It wasn't an easy shot with a handgun or MP5, but not something I hadn't pulled off before. Moreover, he had no idea I had him in my sights. He and his men had been so intent of getting out of the way of the Russian rockets that they had totally ignored where we were and what we were up to.

"No, Sharma. My deal with the Russians was that Soleiman would be theirs. I wouldn't want to piss off nine crazy Russians armed with anti-tank rockets."

He laughed and I had another idea.

"Stand up and wave at that Saudi clown."

The smile disappeared from his face.

"Sharma, get up and wave to your husband. Come on, do something to distract him."

"Fuck you, Sen."

That was the first time Sharma had called me anything other than major and the first time he had sworn at me. I guess that marked a new low in our relationship, and if we both made it out alive and were together on that flight back to Delhi, I would be traveling with two co-passengers who hated my guts. I couldn't really blame him. Being shot was no fun, even when you were wearing a Kevlar vest. Unlike in the movies, bulletproof vests didn't magically make you invulnerable to bullets. They basically dissipate some of the energy from the bullet which prevents the bullet from penetrating your body. Something to do with Kevlar fibers and how tightly they are bound together. Nevertheless, when you're shot by a round coming at you at near supersonic speed, you will likely be knocked off your feet. I know from experience. Also from experience, it hurts like hell, and you'll be sporting a nasty bruise at best and perhaps even cracked ribs or bones if you're shot with a handgun. If you're shot with a high-caliber rifle, then vest or not, you're likely dead. Sharma was glaring at me, clearly refusing to play along.

Well, too bad. Sometimes you had to put the mission first. So, I took out my phone, opened the sound recording app and pressed play.

"Baba!"

Everyone below seemed to look up at once at the child's voice and Soleiman screamed out to me.

"Let go of my son, you monster."

That was a bit rich, for a wife-beating, jihadi-funding, terrorist-loving son of a bitch to call me a monster, but I let that pass and instead put Georgie up over the rampart and then joined Georgie in leaning out, looking straight at Soleiman.

"Soleiman, your son is here as is his favorite toy. You may not give a damn about your men but I'm sure you care about your son. Put down your weapons and surrender to these men and your son will be safe."

He spat at me.

"You are a very poor negotiator. I give myself up to these unknown thugs, and I die somewhere while you take my son away."

"I have no intention of keeping your son, but here's a trade for you. Give yourself up and your son will be off safely with your wife."

"I killed that bitch."

I kicked Sharma hard on the shin and he stood up, wearing his burqa, cringing as if he feared being shot again by Soleiman.

"She's alive, Soleiman."

Soleiman raised his gun at me, and I could hear the Russian rifles snap into place.

"What is your problem? You called me here to make a deal, asking me to help with some enemies of yours in return for my wife and son. Then you shoot at us, these men attack us. Why should I trust anything you say?"

I just kept staring at Soleiman.

"You're a fine one to talk of trust. You said you wanted your wife and son back and the moment you saw your wife, you tried to kill her."

Vasilyev's voice boomed across the courtyard.

"You listen to me, you child-murdering, camel-fucking prince. We are running out of time and patience. Give up or we come in. We'll lose a man or two, but we will slit all your throats."

Soleiman looked at Vasilyev, who was about to say something else. However, he never got a chance to finish his sentence because the man next to him went down, his head torn apart by a bullet from behind.

***

Raza pulled me down.

"Major, who the hell are these now?"

A dozen black-clad men had come in silently, presumably ditching their vehicles far away and coming on foot, undetected. There was a sniper with a long gun with a suppressor attached, crouched near the wreckage of a Saudi SUV. He was the man who had taken Vasilyev's man down, while his comrades, armed with M-4 carbines were streaming into the village.

"Raza, I'd say the ISI sent in its A-team. SSG commandos would be my guess."

As the courtyard below exploded into mayhem as the Russians, Saudis and Pakistanis began firing at each other, Raza, Sharma and I sat side by side, our backs pressed against the wall.

"What are your orders, Sir?"

I looked at Sharma and couldn't help but laugh. From calling me by my name and asking me to fuck off to asking me for orders and calling me sir, he had clearly had a big change of heart. Being in combat with bullets flying all around you can do that to you.

'We kill every single Saudi and Pakistani we can. Just don't shoot the Russians.'

I tossed Sharma a Glock after inserting a fresh clip. He looked at the gun in his hand.

"Major, I'll probably do more harm than good."

I shrugged and peered over the rampart at the mayhem unfolding below. The Pakistanis had fanned out, flanking the Russians. Both sets of men were exceptionally trained and after another Russian had gone down to the first salvo, Vasilyev had rallied his men and taken cover and the two groups were shooting at each other. Soleiman and his men were now crouched behind cover, perhaps wondering what mess they had got stuck in. I saw a Pakistani move out from cover to try and get a better line of fire at the Russians and I took him down with a burst from my MP5 that raked his back. Yes, shooting a man in the back and all that, but in real combat, you toss chivalry out the window. You kill the guy in front of you as quickly and as efficiently as you can.

That first kill told me something. The Pakistanis, thinking they were coming into get me and Raza, had not put on vests. That overconfidence would be their undoing. I picked up another target and put him down with another burst before I ducked to reload. The Pakistanis had no idea we were on top of the fort, and they now turned to meet this new threat.

That was when Vasilyev went Rambo on all of

us. He leaped out, singing words in Russian whose meaning was lost on all of us other than his comrades, firing his weapon on full auto. Two Pakistanis spun around, tossed aside like rag dolls, as Vasilyev threw his rifle aside, and took out his handgun to shoot another Pakistani dead. A couple of Pakistani soldiers tried to bring their weapons to bear on Vasilyev when a Saudi guard stumbled out, almost falling on the sand. What the fuck was this man thinking? The Pakistanis, presuming him to be a threat, pivoted and cut him down, just before three or four Russians fired at once, felling the Pakistanis.

The Pakistanis were professionals, well-trained and motivated, but they were not stupid or suicidal maniacs. They had come in with a clear brief that they were to take me and Raza and had perhaps taken the attack to the Russians thinking they were Indian security forces there to take Raza into custody.

They had not bargained on being caught up in a firefight with mad, singing Russians or suicidal Saudi Royal Guards. They had already lost more than half their number and to give them further cause to reconsider their choices, I aimed at the sniper, who was standing outside the gate, wondering what the hell he and his buddies had got into. Two bursts and he went down, screaming. That did it for the Pakistanis, and they began to stream out of the fort. I took aim at one of them and put my gun down. No, it was okay to kill them when we were engaged in combat. Now, they just wanted to get the hell away, which suited me just fine. Too bad for him that others didn't share that sentiment because a Russian shot him and another of his buddies in the back before the last three Pakistanis ran behind a sand dune and we heard the sound of engines as their dune buggies sped away.

I looked down and saw that the three Saudi Royal Guards still left alive were kneeling, their hands behind their heads as the Russians stood over them.

Where the hell was Soleiman?

"Major, watch..."

Raza never completed that sentence as he careened into me, and into the path of the bullet that had been meant for me. He was hit on the shoulder and went down at my feet, and I saw Soleiman, standing just a few feet from me, a gun in his hand.

***

"Where is my son?"

I pointed to Georgie, lying near my feet.

"He's safe, Soleiman. You didn't think I'd get a small kid in the middle of a gunfight, did you?"

The gun was now pointed at my face.

"Where is he? Who's paying you to get me? Did one of my brothers put you up to this? How are the Russians involved? Do they want to get me for ransom?"

The man was clearly in a panic and had no idea what my involvement in his affairs was. But then, he had so many skeletons in his cupboard that he would do well to be paranoid about which country's intelligence services would be out to get him.

"Soleiman, there's no way out of this other than for you to surrender."

He spat at my feet.

"Idiot, I am Soleiman, prince and heir to the throne of the house of Saud. I do not surrender to gangsters and rogue soldiers."

"I'd say these are just fair consequences for the things you've done."

"Consequences? How can this be the consequence for what I've done?"

"Maybe you should have thought of those consequences before you funded fine people like Benevolence International who went on to pay for the murders of children, or for that matter, funding Al Qaeda bastards who killed innocents across many countries."

His eyes narrowed as he took in the significance of what I was saying. His little secret was no longer such a secret anymore. He looked at Sharma, kneeling on the floor behind me.

"You bitch!"

He was about to fire at Sharma when Raza grabbed his leg, unbalancing him. I leaped across Raza's prone body and into Soleiman, sending both of us tumbling down the short flight of stairs behind him. Both of us hit the wall, landing pretty hard and while I was the first to get up, Soleiman was the first to strike.

He had lost his gun in the melee, but he had whipped out a curved dagger and slashed at me, aiming at my stomach. I managed to deflect the cut by sweeping my left hand in a downward arc, but when I took a step back to gain some space, I saw that I had been cut on my hand. Soleiman now had a crazed look in his eyes. By now he knew that he wasn't getting out of this place, that his days of dreaming about power and riches in the upper echelons of Saudi royalty were over. So, he took all that hate, all that hopelessness and channeled it into the one thing he still could do- kill me.

He advanced on me, swinging his dagger in lazy circles, and suddenly lunged forward, dagger aimed at my chest. I tried to block by taking a step back and bringing my right hand across my body, only to realize it was a feint as he stopped in mid-stroke and raised the dagger, reversing the grip in his hand, bringing it down towards me. I changed my own position, now pivoting slightly to the left and bringing my right hand up to block the blow. As I did, I felt the sting of a cut. I grabbed near his wrist with my right hand and brought my left hand up on the opposite side of his arm, near the forearm. I twisted both in a clockwise motion, adding my body weight to the equation by rotating my hips in the same direction. Soleiman had two choices at that moment. The smarter play would have been to not try and defy the laws of physics and go through with my throw, rolling on the ground to quickly come back up to fight me. He would retain his dagger and all I would have done is brought some time. But I suppose whoever had trained Soleiman hadn't covered that in the syllabus or perhaps years of beating on nobody other than his wife had dulled his skills.

As a result, he tried to resist and wrench his hand back. I slid my left arm up his arm, now resting the hard bone of my elbow on the joint.

Simple physics. Every action has an equal and opposite reaction. I was quite a bit bigger than Soleiman, with at least a dozen kilos in body weight on him. I was bringing a lot of that weight to focus on a very narrow part of his body, specifically with one hand on the bone known as the ulna near the wrist and the other on the bone known as the radius near the forearm. There was no way Soleiman could generate enough force to resist it, but he tried. All that pressure was felt on a very narrow part of his arm, and something had to give, and it did.

I heard a snapping noise as his elbow was dislocated. I let go of his arm as he staggered back, dropping the dagger, his eyes wide in pain. He was staring at his elbow, which was now bent at a strange angle.

I looked him in the eye, and he shrank back. I know what he saw. He saw death.

"Not so tough anymore, prince? I bet you won't be hitting a woman with that arm again."

He tried to say something but then he thought better of it.

"I am a rich man. I can give you more money than you could imagine. You and your Russian friends can all become very rich men. Let me go."

I advanced on him, and he shrank back against the wall, fear in his eyes. I would never get to tell Aisha this, and perhaps she would never want to know such details, but perhaps she would have relished seeing the man who had beaten her, tortured her, reduced to this quivering mess in front of me.

"Major, don't kill him. My bosses would love to have a chat with him."

Vasilyev was standing right behind me, a huge hand on my shoulder. He was a comrade in this mission, but I knew he was under his own orders from his own bosses back in Moscow. I also got a feeling that he wouldn't hesitate to kill me if I came in the way of those orders. He stood next to me and took off his mask, glaring at Soleiman.

"So, this is the camel-fucking prince who murdered little children."

Soleiman perhaps still thought Vasilyev and his men were Russian mobsters or guns for hire, so he tried his luck.

"I don't know who you are, but I am wealthy

beyond your imagination. I can make you and all your friends very rich. Let me go."

Vasilyev spat in his face and Soleiman recoiled back.

"Who I am, you motherfucker, is a former Spetsnaz officer who carried dozens of dead babies out of Beslan."

Understanding dawned on Soleiman, as he realized he was not just being kidnapped for ransom or set up for a hit by a rival prince. He lunged forward in a desperate attempt to get away. I sidestepped him and caught his left hand in a lock using my right hand. I looked up at Vasilyev.

"I get the fact that you need the fucker alive. Your bosses will get lots of goodies out of him and they may well have interesting things to share with the Americans. But tell me something, Vasilyev."

He raised an eyebrow, wondering what I had in mind.

"Do you really need him with his hands intact?"

He roared in laughter and a couple of his men who had come up behind him also laughed.

I put my left hand on Soleiman's shoulder and levered his arm up using my right hand. He began screaming. I brought my face close to his ear.

"This is for Aisha."

Then I broke his arm.

***

EPISODE NINE

FORM 42

Sitting together in the plane, we must have made for quite a sight. Raza had a neck brace, and his left hand was in a sling. Sharma's bandages around his chest weren't visible under his shirt but he too had a neck brace and had somehow managed to cut his hand while falling after being shot and his right hand was heavily bandaged. On my part, both my forearms were bandaged, courtesy of Soleiman and his dagger. The bandages and treatments had been done in a hurry by a doctor the Indian Embassy knew and used, because we couldn't go to a hospital, not knowing whether they would report it to the cops, and we'd spend the night in jail instead of flying back to Delhi.

The air hostess took one look at the three of us and smiled broadly.

"It seems the three of you have been in an accident. I do hope you're feeling better. Let me know if I can do anything to help."

Sharma, who had the aisle seat, grinned at her. As far I knew, he was unmarried, she was cute, and he had thrown back three neat whiskeys at the airport bar before boarding the flight. I was in the window seat and leaned over Raza towards the air hostess.

"Ma'am, we're on official government business and have had a pretty rough day. My friends have been shot and I've been cut. Just get us a whole bunch of drinks as soon as we take off and we'll be okay."

She looked at me in alarm and skittered off, whispering to her colleagues, pointing to us.

"Ever the charming gentleman, Major."

"Fuck off, Raza."

He kept looking straight, but chuckled.

"Don't be so grateful to me for saving your life."

I was about to say something snarky back in return but held back, knowing he had a point.

"Well, thank you. But why would you try and save my life by putting yourself at risk?"

Raza tried to act nonchalant.

"I was wearing a vest, remember?"

"Fuck off, Raza. I don't think you knew with certainty that the bullet wouldn't hit your neck or head. So why did you do it?"

He squirmed in his seat.

"Major, you were my ticket to staying alive."

Then he paused and looked at me.

"Everyone else there, part of that mess we just

escaped from, was there for themselves. I was trying to stay alive, Soleiman wanted his kid and his secrets safe, the Russians wanted Soleiman, the Pakistanis wanted me dead, but what were you there for? You were the one person there trying to do things for others- help Aisha and her son get away, finish your mission by getting me to Delhi. People like you are dangerous, but also rare. It would be a shame if someone like you dies in the middle of nowhere like that."

I turned and looked at him. Raza was a rogue, a criminal and had made his choices long ago for which he would pay. However, he was a man, and I had long learned that the world is not inhabited by heroes and villains, but by ordinary men who make their own choices. Very few people are inherently evil, but they become who they are as a result of those choices.

"Raza, thank you. Not just for saving my life but for helping convince Ali to get Aisha and Amir away."

He caught my gaze.

"I may be a lousy citizen, but I am a good judge of character. I wish you and Aisha had met under different circumstances. I could sense the chemistry, and I think you would have been good together."

I smiled ruefully.

Yes, that was the story of anyone's life, wasn't it? A collection of what-ifs punctuated by the choices we made and the things we actually did. No point really pondering over what might have been. Aisha and I could never be together, but I was happy we got to share some time together, that our lives intersected when they did. By now, she and Amir would be on their flight and all I had to remind me of the time we spent together was Georgie, right now nestled on my lap.

"Major, this will get tricky. Let me do the talking."

I wondered what Sharma was talking about, and then I followed his gaze to the front of the plane.

There were three Emirati cops carrying automatic weapons, and leading them, a very pissed-off looking Sharekh.

***

The air hostesses tried telling Sharekh that the plane was about to taxi to the runway, but Sharekh wasn't even looking at them.

He was looking straight at me.

He and his men walked straight towards me, and I could literally feel every single passenger turn to look at us. The air hostess whom I'd asked for drinks was giving me a slightly betrayed look. Perhaps she thought that far from being government officers as I had said, we were terrorists or criminals on the run. When Sharekh reached us, he whispered to his men, and they walked back to the front of the plane. Sharekh motioned for Sharma to get up and sat down in his place.

"Sharekh, I can explain and get authorization from

my government."

Sharekh just looked up at Sharma and shook his head.

"I want to talk to the major."

He turned to me, and Raza slunk back in his seat, trying to make himself invisible.

"So, Major Sen. You're in Dubai for a couple of days on what I'm told is a very routine and simple mission to fly this gentleman back to India."

That had been the plan, indeed. Sharekh leaned towards me.

"Instead, we have four men killed at the hotel including two of my men, a shoot-out reported at the Spice Market, two Pakistani embassy men killed on the highway, and now a total massacre at Hatta. They're saying there are at least a dozen bodies there- including Saudi Royal Guards and what look like active-duty Pakistani army men. Do you have anything to say?"

I held his gaze. He mentioned no dead Russians, which meant Vasilyev had taken his dead with him and left no traces of his involvement.

"Sharekh, the men of yours who were killed at the hotel were good men, and I had nothing to do with their deaths. I killed the two bastards who killed them and were trying to take Raza. You should know that, if you haven't figured that out already."

He nodded.

"For that I hold no grudges against you, but Dubai

is one of the safest places in the world. Our murder rate has been between 0.1 and 0.3 per hundred thousand people. That means between three and ten murders a year. You come here and the body count exceeds that in a day or two! That takes some doing."

I was continuing to look at Sharekh's eyes. I was not compelled to say anything to him. Of course, Sharma had a diplomatic passport and at worst would get expelled. I had no such protection and could be hauled off to a prison, but if Sharekh had wanted to arrest me, he would have already done that.

"I'm just a soldier doing my mission, Sharekh. Those men on the highway were not here to strengthen cultural ties between the Emirates and Pakistan. I'm sure you found guns in the wreckage and a simple background check would perhaps show they'd served in the army or ISI, but I suspect you've already done that."

Sharekh just nodded again.

"I suppose your government won't care about a few dead Pakistanis, either. They stick their noses into places where they don't belong, and they should expect their noses to be bloodied once in a while. You're in the same line of business I'm in, so I suspect you know that."

He nodded and I kept going, now clearer on what he wanted.

"Soleiman."

He nodded.

"Major, he is not just a Saudi prince but someone who was close to our rulers. What will people say if they think we cannot even protect our honored guests? For someone like him to disappear is a big embarrassment. Your government has cleared everything else up with us, but they have no idea how he was involved with you and what happened to him. I can only surmise you know more than you're saying because all those Saudi Royal Guards showed up dead at Hatta, where the Indian government told us you were arranging to get Raza into Sharma's custody."

"Sharekh, I don't know where Soleiman is."

"I didn't say you knew where he was, Major, but perhaps you know who took him. Tell me that and you can go home."

He didn't need to say what would happen if I didn't say who had taken Soleiman. I guessed I'd find out first-hand whether Emirati jails were as crappy as people said they were. If I told him the truth, I'd get into deep trouble back home, as the Indian government had no idea I'd done a side deal with Russian mercenaries to have a Saudi prince kidnapped on foreign soil. That kind of thing tends to make for interesting newspaper headlines and short careers. Sharekh clearly felt that I needed more encouragement, so he helpfully added some more information.

"For now, this is all between my government and yours. We're allies, trying to keep this quiet and resolve it in a friendly manner. If the Saudis get involved any more than they are and learn you may have something to do with whatever fate has befallen Soleiman, things will get more complicated. So please tell me all you know about his whereabouts."

The one silver lining in an otherwise pretty messed up situation for me was that at least he made no mention of me sleeping with, or helping a Saudi princess run away. I think the punishment for adultery in Saudi Arabia was death and given I had killed so many of their men and made one of their princes disappear into Russian custody, I suspected they would cut me into pieces. I mean, for God's sake, they had supposedly done that to a bloody Western journalist in their consulate. For someone like me, I could expect even worse. I kept a straight face, and kept looking at Sharekh, trying to think of what to say, wishing I were not just a dumb soldier and some sort of suave spy who could make up shit to get out of a situation like this.

Suddenly, Raza spoke up, coughing gently to get our attention.

"Sharekh, the young man has no idea. Soleiman was after me because I knew all about some of his financial dealings and how he had supported some nasty men in Syria and Iraq with his money and later double-crossed them by not sending them funds when they desperately needed them once American missiles and bombs started falling."

Damn! Raza should have been a novelist. Where had this twist come from? However he had conjured it up, he clearly had Sharekh's interest now as he continued.

"The Pakistanis were of course after me, keen to stop me from getting into Indian hands. Soleiman saw his chance to shut me up before too many people knew that our suave, fancy, westernized prince was in bed with masked thugs who liked to cut off people's heads on camera. Some of those friends he had stiffed must have come to know of his presence here and got him. There were a bunch of masked men with guns who came and took him away. If the Saudis want him back, they may have to look somewhere in Iraq, Syria or perhaps Yemen. But this young man next to me has no idea where Soleiman is. He was just doing his job and trying to keep me alive."

"You're defending the man who's taking you to prison?"

Raza stared at Sharekh with a small smile.

"I'm defending the man who kept me alive when nobody else would or could. By the way, I doubt your government would want to be publicly associated with the kind of men who may have taken Soleiman, so it may be best to lie low and let the Saudis figure this one out. Believe me, they've dealt with men like these before."

Sharekh looked at me for what seemed to be a long time and finally shook his head.

"You are bad news, Major. I wish I could say I hope

to see you again, but it may be in your best interests to not come to this part of the world for some time."

With that he left with his men. I breathed a huge sigh of relief and as the plane began to taxi to the runway, I called the air hostess over. After the day I had, all I wanted was a stiff drink. Even as I motioned to her, I glanced at Sharma. Technically, I was still on duty, and getting drunk on duty would add to my already long list of career-ending actions. Sharma smiled at me.

"You deserve a few drinks, Major. Don't worry, I'll keep watch and for any of the bureaucrats who ask, I'll say I relieved you of duty to help you take care of your wounds and took charge of the prisoner."

Good man, Sharma. The air hostess was looking curiously at me now, perhaps wondering if I was one of the good guys or bad guys.

"Ma'am, please can you get us all large whiskies on the rocks as soon as you can?"

A few minutes later, she was back with the drinks, and I emptied my glass before asking for a refill. Raza laughed out loud.

"I thought we'd at least raise a toast."

"Next drink, Raza. I needed that one to just get my hands to stop shaking and my heart to stop racing. You do realize how close I came to being cut to ribbons by some Saudi butcher. Thank you for that save."

As my drink arrived, Raza raised his glass to mine and Sharma's.

"To being a team. The most unlikely team ever assembled, but a team, nevertheless. And to our leader, the good major here. A fine soldier whose legacy will be saving all our asses, even if that meant tripling the murder rate in Dubai."

We all laughed. It wasn't that funny, but we all had nervous energy to burn off, and with the next drink I raised a toast of my own.

"To Raza, all round rogue and criminal. May he serve the punishment he deserves for what he's done, yet may he discover the man within, who is capable of better things, of being a better man, glimpses of whom I've seen."

Raza smiled and met my glass with his own. The last toast was to Sharma who turned red with embarrassment when I made the toast.

"To Sharma, fearless spy extraordinaire, and the sexiest IB agent ever in a burqa."

As the plane took to the sky, I saw the lights of an airliner in the distance. Wouldn't it be cool if that was the plane Aisha and Amir were on? I knew that was a remote possibility, but who knew? Especially four drinks down, who knew?

I held Georgie up to the window and we both waved goodbye.

***

It was three in the morning when we exited the airplane, and all three of us were more than slightly high, and I think at one point, Raza was holding my arm for support as we walked through the air bridge. Sharma, good officer that he was, had held off after two drinks, but after having been shot, getting hardly any sleep, already a few drinks down at the airport bar, being topped off with two more whiskies meant that he was only slightly more sober than us.

To my horror, and presumably that of Sharma, in front of us stood Srini, my boss; Sharma's boss, a gentleman I had never met but knew to be the Director of the IB, and four tough looking young men, dressed in civilian clothes, but carrying sub machine guns. They grinned when they saw me. Unni, Kishore, Bahadur and Pratap. All Unit 22 boys who worked in Operations, all of whom had served with me on the frontlines and had come through for me during the troubles we had faced the previous year. Along with them was Salil, who walked up to me, sniffed and grinned.

"I see you guys had a good time."

I leaned towards him and whispered.

"This is as career threatening as it gets, isn't it?"

Next thing I knew, Srini was standing in front of me, his hands on my shoulders.

"Good to have you back, my boy. Good to have you back. That was some adventure you had."

"I'm sorry, I hadn't expected all of you here.

Otherwise, I may have had one drink less."

He roared with laughter and the Ops boys and Salil joined in. The IB Director, a desk bound spy, who hadn't been in the army like the rest of us, looked on with faint distaste, but Srini clapped me on the shoulder again.

"You can have all the bloody drinks you want, Sen. All the drinks you want."

Then he walked over to Raza and peered at him.

"For a man who's likely to spend the rest of his life in prison, you seem to be in good enough spirits, Raza."

Raza, because he was drunk and perhaps his relief at being alive and on Indian soil overpowering the minor detail that he was here as a prisoner, for reasons best known to him, saluted Srini.

"Raza reporting for duty, Sir."

The Ops boys laughed again, and this time I joined in, concluding that Raza was much more fun when he had a few drinks in him. Sharma stepped forward, perhaps trying to make a good impression on his boss and realized too late that he was carrying Georgie. How Georgie made his way from me to him was a minor detail which was lost in the haziness of the many drinks we'd had.

Salil steered me away from the crowd of passengers and whispered into my ears.

"You need to get some sleep, buddy. I'll get you to a guest house. Sleep, freshen up and then spend tomorrow at home."

"What about Raza? Will he be safe?"

"The whole top brass is here to take him in. Don't worry. Nobody can get to him now."

I woke up at nine, without clothes and with Georgie next to me.

What a night.

"Georgie, I do hope next time you keep me from drinking so much."

My phone rang and I saw that it was Ma.

"Salil told me you were back in town but that you were debriefing and would come in the morning."

I sent a silent thanks to Salil. Every man should have a friend who can pass off his sleeping off a hangover as professional debriefing to his mother.

"Ma, it's good to be home. I'm coming over right now."

***

"Ma, if I eat any more, I swear I'll burst."

That did not deter Ma from putting another egg in front of me. To be honest, my objections were pretty half-hearted. Ma's special recipe, egg coated in all sorts of masalas, crumbed and then deep fried, had been a favorite of mine and some of my earliest memories had been of her cooking in the kitchen, telling me about her day in school.

"Eat, Aadi. You look like you've had a pretty eventful office trip."

Ma was a soldier's wife and a soldier's mother, so she knew better than to ask what I had been through, but equally, she knew what had happened to me. Both Baba and I had come back home from deployments with injuries, and she knew by looking at the bandages that I had been slashed on both arms.

"Did they give you a Tetanus shot for the cuts?"

"Yes, Ma."

"Did you achieve what you set out to?"

I thought that one over. I had set out to get Raza into our custody, and I had achieved that, but through a detour that I had never expected. I wondered where Aisha and Amir were and whether they were safe.

"I did everything I could, Ma. Some things turned out well, others, I just hope they do."

She stroked my hair.

"That's the best one can do, son. By the way, I won a little victory of my own."

I looked at her, seeing the smile on her face and I exhaled in relief, knowing what she was going to say, but wanting to hear the words out aloud.

"The scan was clear."

I had tears in my eyes when I hugged her.

"Wait for a second, Ma."

I went into the kitchen and came back with a bottle of wine which I poured into two glasses. Then I raised a toast.

"May we keep winning all our battles and live long."

My mother, being a soldier's widow and mother to a soldier who had spent his whole career going into harm's way, knew better than to tempt fate, so she raised a toast of her own.

"May we live well in the time we have been given."

***

My respite was short-lived because that evening I was back at work. Srini and Salil were the only ones there and Sharma joined us in a few minutes. Srini looked harried, and when one realizes that he was a career government officer who was now having to contemplate acting against his political boss, it was perfectly understandable.

"Raza is singing like a canary. I have no doubts the government will be lenient on him and perhaps give him a nice, cozy cell to serve out his sentence for the rest of his life."

"Being in prison for the rest of his life doesn't sound too cozy, Sir."

Srini grinned.

"You haven't seen the VIP cells some people get. TV, Internet, a library, better food than the normal prisoners."

"That's a lot to give to a man who has innocent blood on his hands and is known to have funded terrorists."

Srini sat down heavily with a sigh.

"Politics, my boy. Politics. If he had dirt on the PM or top leaders in his party, I doubt people would be so considerate towards him. But he has lots of dirt on leaders in the opposition which he's offering up very easily. Makes the PM look good and the opposition look bad. Very convenient with major state elections coming up in a couple of months."

I thought back to Raza and some of the names he had taken. He was being shrewd, but then I had expected nothing less of him. He had dirt on all kinds of people, but he had calculated rightly that if he offered up information which helped the PM and the government in their political agenda, he would be treated well. Perhaps they would even spin his tale as that of a small-time crook who had been manipulated by evil politicians. He knew that if he started taking some of the names he could, he wouldn't just have a less comfortable cell, he'd probably be hanging to death. I had spent enough time with Raza to see that he wasn't just an ogre, but a man who had made bad choices, which he needed to pay for. Part of me, the part that had seen him capable of putting his own life in danger to save mine, felt relieved that he was getting off easy. Another part of me, the one which had vowed to hunt down enemies of the state and those who threatened the innocent, felt it wasn't fair. Srini must have read the expression on my face. I may be a decent soldier, but I am a terrible actor.

"Sen, that's life. Sometimes, justice isn't quite what you hope for, but at least he's out of action and won't be causing any more damage, and we will use the intel he gives us on his Pakistani and jihadi connections to do some real damage to our enemies."

There was one name which Srini had not mentioned.

"What about our man? Surely, he won't get away after arranging attacks on us in Dubai and all the stuff he has done over the years?"

Srini leaned forward.

"That's the reason I've called all of you here this late. Raza actually took his name."

This time it was Sharma who responded.

"If he's only taking names which help the government politically, why would he take this name? Surely, calling out a serving minister who is spoken of as a potential PM aspirant can't be good for the government?"

Srini strummed his fingers on the table.

"Raza is smart, very smart. Raza knows he set up hits on him from what you went through together in Dubai. So perhaps he wants payback, but he is also shrewd. This man had defected to the ruling party only a couple of years ago, and it allows the government to say that his past misdeeds and connections with the drug trade and terrorists were something they had no idea about, that all of those happened when he was in the opposition."

"What's he doing, Sir? I'm sure he suspects Raza will out him. He was desperate enough to arrange those attacks on us."

Srini looked at me.

"That's where we have a problem. The man is missing."

"Missing? How can a minister go missing?"

Srini was strumming his fingers on the table again. When the normally stoic Srini did stuff like this, you knew he was anxious and running out of ideas.

"We're working on it, Sen. The problem is what do we do when we manage to find him?"

That was weird and I wasn't the only one who thought so. Salil put something in front of Srini.

"Sir, looking at the transcripts of Raza's confession, we have enough to put this scumbag away for a long time. He's not just paid the underworld to do his dirty work, including murdering a political opponent, but we now know that he was on the ISI's payroll to provide information on our armed forces' movements."

I took the paper and scanned it, my blood boiling with every line I read.

"Sir, this bastard deserves to hang. He's sold out our nation and directly or indirectly led to the deaths of many of our boys."

Srini looked up at me, and I could see a strange look in his eyes.

"You see, Sen, our intel is that the ISI is trying

to get him out of the country. Even if we track him down, we'd have to confront them and that would get very ugly, very quickly. The PM is trying to arrange a meeting on the sidelines of the UN meeting next week with the Pakistani leadership to get them to ratchet down their rhetoric, and he's not very keen on our policemen getting into a shooting match with Pakistani officials on our soil. Likely those ISI bastards will have diplomatic cover, and this would get very messy if we tried to tackle it through official channels."

I now saw why Srini had called me in so late. I put the paper down in front of him.

"Sir, get me the Unit 22 boys. I know they're all based in Delhi now, and you could pull them back from their current duties to Unit 22. We'll handle this on the quiet. Nothing official about it."

I had half expected Srini to say that we couldn't just pull off missions like that on our soil against Pakistani officials, but I was surprised when he said nothing. I didn't expect him to say yes or to give me anything in writing. I knew how missions like these worked. Plausible deniability. It wasn't anything personal that Srini had against me, but the way of the world. If we succeeded, nobody would hear of it. If we failed, then the government would say it had nothing to do with it. I was fine with that. I had played by those rules many times, and as long as that led to the bad guys being put into the ground or behind bars, it was all worth it.

"Sen, finding him will take time. They wouldn't risk the exposure of hiding him in their embassy but I'm sure they have him in a safe house somewhere. Sharma, please get your IB contacts spinning."

"Yes, Sir. We have enough people who would help us for money or patriotism and anything as big as this will leave ripples that will be noticed. I'll get on it and will be in touch."

As Sharma left to get to work, Salil and I looked at each other. We were probably thinking the same thing.

"Just one question, Sir. If I find that bastard and he resists, do I have authorization to take him dead or alive?"

If Srini had surprised me earlier with his tacit approval for me and the boys to go after our man on the quiet, he shocked me with the paper he slipped on the table in front of me.

"A letter from the PM himself authorizing you to take any action you deem fit as the tactical commander on the ground. Getting him in custody would be preferable but he would understand if things didn't work out that way."

I just nodded.

It was time to go to war.

***

It was two in the morning when the call came. Sharma had been his usual efficient self, and his contacts had come through big time. It was hard to move someone as high profile as a minister through underground channels without getting some attention, I suppose. When the call came, Salil was sitting next to me at our safe house, together with Unni, Kishore, Pratap and Bahadur. Salil smirked.

"Anything's possible when you pay someone big bucks for information. Enough money to buy a new house, perhaps."

I was a soldier, but not a spy, so this was all still pretty new to me.

"You mean just to pass on this kind of info, someone could make that much money in one night?"

When he nodded, I looked at the boys.

"We made the wrong career choice. We get paid peanuts and we run the chance of getting killed."

Unni was the quiet sort, lean like a marathon runner and he just nodded. Pratap was big, a few inches taller than me and built like a wrestler. He laughed.

"Sir, but then we wouldn't have the satisfaction of taking out the bastards who need to be taken out."

Point.

"Boys, everyone geared up?"

We all checked our own gear and that of our buddies. We were not wearing our unit uniforms, given the clandestine nature of the mission we were on, but were all wearing track suits. We were each wearing Kevlar vests under our jackets, helmets with built in night vision googles over one eye, tactical knee and elbow pads, and each had a Glock 17 handgun on a shoulder holster, a Tavor assault rifle and the boys also had a commando knife. I had my trusted khukri, one which had belonged to a buddy I had once lost in combat.

Salil watched me in silence as I sent a message to Ma that I would be out for the night on a job, closed my eyes, thinking of Baba and his final deployment. If I fell, I wanted to go a hero as he had done.

"You okay, Sen?"

When I opened my eyes and looked at Salil, he flinched. He had usually seen me in the office, but now he saw me for who I really was- a soldier, in the company of other soldiers, about to go to war. The boys were looking at me expectantly, and I realized what I loved the most about serving with men like them was not just the adrenaline rush of going into harm's way for a mission we believed in, it was the fact that these men would do so, fully trusting me, without even asking me what the mission was. That put a lot of responsibility on my shoulders, but that also made me love them all the more. It was time to tell them what we were about to do.

"Ready, boys?"

Their voices boomed out as one.

"Ready, Sir!"

"Who are we, boys?"

"We are Para Archers! We are the Special Group!"

All five of us had come in from the Para Special Forces of the Indian army and joined the airborne branch of the SFF called the Para Archers. When I moved to the Special Group and was asked to choose some of my men to come with me, I had hand-picked these four. These four were also the ones I had pulled into Unit 22 a few months ago when we had been on the trail of assassins out to get the US President.

"Damn right we are! We are also now part of an even more elite family all our own. Unit 22. Maybe after this action, they'll rotate you all back to your regular units and shut us down to avoid any leaks about the mission we are on. But tonight, we have a unit to call our own. A family of our own. Unit 22. Nobody fucks with our country while we are around."

They growled in assent as I continued.

"There are Pakistani men on our soil, trying to take away a son of a bitch who has betrayed us. A minister who has been on the Pakistani payroll and has led to many deaths, both of innocent civilians and of our comrades. Here he is."

I could see widened eyes as they took in who our target was, but they said nothing till Bahadur, the most aggressive of the lot, tapped the photo.

"This motherfucker is a dead man."

I knew my boys and I knew that if I unleashed them with a kill order, they would shoot to kill, so I added one last point.

"We have to take him dead or alive, though if it has to be dead, I take the call and ideally I take the shot."

The men nodded and I knew they understood. If anything went wrong afterwards and we were hung out to dry for killing a minister, I would be the one taking the fall.

I distributed the earpieces we would all be wearing, to stay connected throughout the mission and we put them on.

Salil was just behind me as we left the safe house.

"Salil, you don't have to come. You do know that, don't you?"

Salil had been in the National Security Guard for a couple of years, so he was extremely well trained, but he had never seen combat and had been in an office for years. The last thing I wanted was for him to get hurt. He grinned.

"Sen, I have no delusions about my ability to take on SSG men in my current level of fitness and with the lack of recent firearms training, but I can help in ways other than pulling triggers."

He pointed to his own earpiece.

"Let me be your spotter and lookout. I'll stay in touch with the boss and Sharma and let you know of any intel we get."

I looked back at the boys.

"Time to hunt."

***

The target was an old warehouse near Noida and if I were a Pakistani officer, who had perhaps served in the SSG, and was operating deep behind enemy lines trying to get someone out, I reckoned I would have a system of watchers and trip wires. So, we got out of our car more than five kilometers away from the target and jogged our way there. At four in the morning, there was nobody on the road, and if anyone saw us, they would perhaps think of us as six fitness fanatics on the road. All our weapons and helmets were in the backpacks on our back, to be put on when we were closer to the target. I whistled to Unni, who nodded and took off in a loping gait which left us far behind. He was the fastest of us and by far the best runner and I wanted him to get a look ahead. It proved to be the right call and a huge stroke of luck for us, when I heard his voice in my earpiece.

"One man, pretending to be jogging. One klick out, headed your way."

"Did he see you?"

"Negative. I was on the other side of the road."

"Are you sure he's a tango?"

"He's got an earpiece and in the five minutes I've

seen him, he's jogged one way then come back and when he thought nobody was looking, he took out a Glock and checked the mag."

That sealed it. I looked at the others around me.

"We've got a live one, as you heard. Pratap, you go grab him. Leave your backpack with me."

Pratap ran on and we followed in a slower jog behind him. A few minutes later as we passed a turn on the road, I heard a short whistle and we turned to the side of the road. Unni and Pratap were there, next to a terrified looking man with his hands tied and Pratap's knife at his throat.

Unni handed me his wallet and I examined it.

"Kind of late for a low-level embassy employee who supposedly assists the cultural attaché to be out for a run, carrying a loaded gun."

He realized that I was the one in charge and began to take on an indignant tone.

"I have diplomatic immunity. You can't just grab me like this. Who are you? If you want to kidnap me, you should know that you won't get away with it."

I took out my khukri from my backpack and held it close to his face. His eyes widened as he saw the wicked, curved blade.

"What you have, my friend, is one chance to tell me how many of your buddies are guarding the fat minister."

His eyes widened as he realized who we were.

"I know nothing."

Wrong answer. Ten minutes later, we were on our way to the target, in full gear. We left our friend bloodied, gagged, naked and tied up on the side of the road. He had told us a fair bit. Everyone talks, especially when they're having pieces of their ear sliced off with the promise that their balls are next.

We ran the last two kilometers at a brisk pace, leaving Salil behind. While he couldn't really keep up with us when it came to running, he was more than doing his bit. As we saw the dark outline of the warehouse ahead of us, his voice came over the earpiece.

"Guys, the turd you caught was ISI. Sharma's sending the IB boys to scoop him up. We also had time to run three of the six names he gave us. All Pak army men, SSG commandoes, no less. Seem to have come in under assumed names under the cover of a cultural exchange program."

"Boys, you heard the man. Six SSG men. Every male you see there who isn't so fat he'll die of a heart attack is a legit target. These boys will be trained well and motivated, so don't try anything fancy. Shoot first, shoot fast, shoot to kill. They don't have night vision and only have handguns, so let's make the most of that edge. I want every single of one of you alive and well so we can drink ourselves silly together when we're done here."

The first to die were two men patrolling the front

door, taken down by suppressed shots from Unni and Pratap. Bahadur was in next, covered by Kishore. I heard the hushed pops of three bursts, and I knew they'd cleared the entrance. Then I was through, with the boys just over my shoulders. So far, four Pakistanis had been taken down without being able to fire a shot. One man came out of a darkened corner. He was trying to see who had come in the darkness while I was seeing him clearly through the ghostly green glow of my night vision. Not fair, and too bad for him. I shot him in the chest with a three-round burst and scanned up the stairs to see another man coming down, gun in hand. He got a shot off, which was absurdly loud in the cocooned interior of the warehouse. I didn't get time to see if he hit anyone or anything but swung my rifle up as he pointed his gun at me. One burst to the chest sent him staggering back and then someone else finished him with another burst that took off his head.

Lesson learned- don't bring a Glock to a Tavor fight.

The boys swept downstairs, just in case our naked friend had been lying while I went up the stairs. I saw him sitting on a dirty mattress on the floor, his hair unkempt, a large suitcase beside him, the room dimly lit by a kerosene lamp next to the mattress.

How the mighty had fallen.

As I approached him, he pointed to the suitcase.

"There are a million dollars in there. Take what you want. Just let me go."

"Too late for that, motherfucker."

When I took off my helmet and knelt in front of him, he shrank back, his eyes widening in recognition.

"Major, I had nothing to do with the Pakistanis for some time. It was all in my past. I can explain."

"Explain sending men to kill me in Dubai."

He swallowed hard.

"It was nothing personal."

I slapped him and he fell back on the mattress.

"Having trained killers sent after you is personal, my friend. And when you betray our country, sell our secrets to the enemy and cause the deaths of good men and women, it is personal."

To my surprise, he smiled.

"Take me in, then. You people think small, which is why you remain small. A government salary, a pension. That's the limit of your ambition. What do you think will happen if I'm taken alive? Do you really think the Prime Minister will commit political suicide by having his Home Minister exposed as a Pakistani spy? He'll make a deal, and I'll retire from politics to spend my years farming or writing a book. Maybe I'll give some scraps of what I know about Pakistani ops here, and they'll actually be grateful for my help."

I just looked at the man in front of me, with his million dollars, his Louis Vuitton shoes, his smug expression, and I hated him. Most of all, I hated the fact that what he was saying was true. Real life was no movie. The bad guys didn't always get what they deserved, and the truth didn't always prevail. Truth was what the politicians, media and corporations wanted you to see. Truth was what was politically expedient and what could be bought. I took out my khukri.

"I spent a fair bit of time with Raza, and he told me all that you did for the Pakistanis. You sold us out many times, but I want to talk about one particular incident where you tipped them off about movements of a special forces unit in Kashmir. An incident where three of our men were captured by a Pakistani Border Action Team and two of them were tortured and beheaded. One got away."

He still didn't know why I was talking about that incident, so I crept closer to him, my face inches from his.

"The two men who were killed were my brothers. I was the one who got away and I didn't come back empty-handed. I came back with three Pakistani heads, all cut with this khukri."

He emitted a low mewing sound, perhaps out of things to say, perhaps realizing nothing he said would make a difference.

"My boss told me to bring you in dead or alive. He said he preferred alive, but you know, I was always bad at following orders."

He began to scream as I moved over him.

***

Ma said nothing the next morning. She knew I had been out on a mission, and she knew that the kind of mission that would take me out all night and bring me back at seven in the morning with dried blood on my hands was not the sort I could tell her anything about. I slept in late, after telling the boys to sleep and get some rest. When I reached the office in the afternoon, Srini and Salil were waiting for me. Srini nodded as I came in.

"Sen, six SSG men gone and one ISI operative captured. Quite a success. I suspect you're going to get another medal for this one, though I know you don't really care. What I was waiting to hear from you was what happened at the end. You were the only one with him."

I sat down in front of Srini after pouring myself some coffee.

"Sir, I confronted the fugitive and asked him to hand himself in. He resisted and during the confrontation, a kerosene lamp in the room was upturned and the room caught fire. I tried to drag him out, but it was too late. The whole warehouse burned down as it had a lot of hay and fertilizers which nearby farmers had stored there."

Srini looked straight into my eyes.

"Yes, it was some fire. The explosion woke up everyone within a few kilometers. Too bad about him. A pity we couldn't get the bastard alive."

The TV was on behind Srini, and I heard the news anchor speaking with a photo on the screen behind him.

"Shocking news coming in this morning. Manoj Kumar Pandey, the Union Home Minister, is reported to have died in an accident early this morning when a fire broke out at an agricultural warehouse near Noida. Mr. Pandey, who came from a wealthy farming family, was reportedly at the warehouse inspecting farm equipment when the accident occurred."

Srini turned off the TV.

"Sen, you're not done yet on this job."

"Sir?"

I could see Salil stifle a grin as Srini continued.

"Paperwork, Sen, paperwork. You need to do a Form 42 on your trip to Dubai and what happened there. With all the mayhem you unleashed, lots of bureaucrats and ministries want to know what happened."

A Form 42. Give me Pakistani SSG men any day over paperwork.

"Sir, I have a medical condition that comes in the way of doing good Form 42s."

Srini looked at me, bewildered.

"It's called Cathisophobia."

Salil could hold it no longer and burst out laughing. Srini shook his head.

"You guys fool around all you want. Just give me a damn Form 42 so I can feed the bureaucratic beast."

"But sir, I can't write what actually happened, can I? I mean, Pandey just supposedly died in a farming accident, so I presume I can't mention what Raza told me."

Srini looked at me with genuine sympathy. I think he realized just how much a fish out of water I was in dealing with bureaucratic shenanigans.

"Sen, I can bet you my pension that nobody will read it. I will put all kinds of confidentiality and need to know tags around it, and the bureaucrats just want to know that your mission was properly authorized and documented, so they can cover their asses if anyone asks about it. Just write what you feel like."

A few minutes later, I was in my office, a steaming cup of coffee next to me as I began typing my Form 42.

It all started when I went to buy a baboon in Dubai.

***

EPISODE TEN

THE SPY WHO LOVED ME

"Ma, where's Georgie?"

She looked at me, eyebrows raised, perhaps wondering if I had finally lost my mind on a Sunday morning as soon as I got up from sleep.

"Last time I checked, Aadi, there have been only two of us living here. So, who is this Georgie?"

I laughed as I responded.

"That toy which came with me from Dubai."

She came close to my bed.

"You never did tell me why you came back with a stuffed monkey."

Where could I begin?

"It's a long story, Ma. I found it during the mission, and he ended up being helpful and the person he belonged to insisted I take him with me."

She shook her head, perhaps knowing better than

to ask me what kind of mission I had been on and what kind of people I had ended up being involved with.

"Well, wherever he came from, he stinks of gunpowder and is really dusty. I checked the label, and it says he's machine washable, so I thought it'd put him along with the laundry."

I got out of bed and took a long, hot shower, thinking that Georgie was likely doing the same inside the washing machine. It had been three days since I had come back, and work was quiet. I mean after all the chaos we had gone through, anything would seem quiet in comparison. Raza was still being grilled by the spooks and in turn was no doubt striking the best bargain he could for himself. Pandey had already disappeared from the headlines, and I could sense that the government was happy to see it that way. Part of me wondered if the PM and his top brass had actually sent me and my boys after Pandey, hoping that we would kill him and remove the inconvenience of having your Home Minister exposed as having been on Pakistani payroll. Far easier to shed a few tears for the camera, to eulogize the fallen patriot than to field uncomfortable questions about why a Pakistani spy was on your Council of Ministers.

When I came out, Ma was holding Georgie in her hands.

"Looks like he skipped his shower, Ma."

"I was trying to take off his t-shirt and I found this

tucked inside. Funny thing was that it was sewed onto the shirt."

As she handed me the object, I saw that it was a USB stick. As Ma left with Georgie, I plugged it into my laptop and saw that there was only one file on it- a video. When I clicked it, my breath caught for a second as I saw Aisha fill the screen. She must have recorded it on her mobile when we were at Ali's place, as I could recognize the walls behind her. Seeing her face gave me almost a physical jolt. I remembered her bright eyes, her smell, her touch. I had to shake myself back to the present and pay attention to what she was saying.

"Aadi, I didn't want us to part ways and for you to later wonder if our time together had meant anything at all. I just wanted you to know that it meant a lot. In a world where so many things aren't what they seem, so many people aren't who they seem, I wanted you to hear straight from me about what is true. Everything I told you about Soleiman is true. Everything I shared about Amir is true, and thanks to you, I and my son will be safe. I also want you to know that what we shared was real, and it meant a lot to me. In the line of work we are in, we meet all kinds of people, and most of them are out to achieve their selfish objectives. You are rare. You did what you did not because it would bring you money, fame, power or accolades. You put yourself at risk to help total strangers. That takes a special kind of man, and that is what attracted me to you. It's a shame that given the lives we lead, we will likely never meet again, but I didn't want these things to remain unsaid. No matter what you learn or hear later, I didn't want you to doubt that these things were true."

Amir jumped into the frame.

"Hi! Be good, Iron Man and take care of Georgie. I've asked him to help you in all your missions!"

Then they were gone.

I just sat there for a long time, thinking about everything Aisha had said. Yes, we could never be together in the long term. Perhaps that was my curse, to meet remarkable women like Amy and Aisha, whom I had very little time with. But then a different thought struck me. How long you spent with someone was less important than how well you spent the time you had together, no matter how short. People could spend a lifetime together without passion, without respect, without love. With both Amy and Aisha, I had met women whom I was not only attracted to, but women who had real strength, real character. I had not managed to save Amy, but Aisha was going to be safe, and it was enough for me to know that.

As I began to get up, something else struck me. Aisha had gone to great lengths to tell me the many things she had told me that were true. She had emphasized that point.

So, what had she told me that was not true?

***

"Murthy, Sen, I wanted you here for a specific reason this morning. Sharma will be here soon."

For Srini to call us in very early on a Monday morning wasn't unusual. The nature of our work was such that we had to be ready to report for duty whenever something came up. After all, terrorists weren't very considerate of others' work life balance. What was unusual was for Srini to insist that we not meet in office, but over breakfast at the Taj. As soon as we both reached the lobby, Salil had whispered to me.

"Boss seems to be feeling particularly generous. Treating us at the Taj?"

I, ever the cynic, had no such delusions.

"More likely feeding us before he throws us into the deep end again."

As we sat around the table making small talk, Sharma joined us, looking equally puzzled at being called for this meeting. After all, he didn't even report into Srini, and under normal circumstances, the bureaucrats lining our offices would have thrown a fit at demanding a proper agenda and a request for inter-agency sharing- the usual political bullshit that kept them happy and got people like us killed in the field. Srini heaped his plate with fruits and yogurt and came back, talking about how he was trying to stay healthy, and making me feel more than a bit guilty about stuffing my plate with eggs, sausages and hash browns.

"Boys, I called you outside of office because I wanted

to tell you personally before you got the paperwork."

Shit. Maybe they were tired of all the trouble I seemed to get into and were finally firing me. The panicked look on Sharma's face told me that I wasn't the only one having such thoughts. Srini caught my glance.

"What's wrong, Sen? What do you think this is about?"

I cleared my throat and took a big sip of coffee, wishing I had something stronger instead.

"Considering I killed a few Pakistani diplomats, beat up some Saudi royal guards, tripled the murder rate in Dubai and then caused the mother of all agricultural accidents, I suppose it would be appropriate to expect to be fired."

He looked at me for a second, checking if I was joking and then he roared in laughter, and kept laughing while Sharma and I looked at each other. Sharma had the same expression that he had when he had been shot at Hatta. An expression which told me that I had fucked him over. I took a couple of deep breaths and waited for Srini to settle down.

"Sen, you are priceless. No, you are not being fired. I personally briefed the PM on what happened in Dubai and then here. And before you worry, I didn't use your Form 42. I don't think he'd appreciate the niceties involved in choosing a baboon lamp in Dubai."

Fuck. So, someone did read that Form 42, and it

had to be my boss. Salil kicked me under the table, enjoying my discomfiture as Srini continued.

"Together with the work you did when the plot against the US President came up, the PM is very impressed. Believe me, he will want to pin another medal on you. Pity you can't be at a parade or receive it with the media around, but your medal collection is going to grow."

The government had given me all sorts of medals over the years, and the only medals I valued were the ones my men received for work they had done. Whether I got a medal or not was not important in and of itself to me, especially if that medal came for a mission where I lost boys. Srini knew that and I knew he would not have called us all here just to talk about medals.

"I've been reflecting on the last few operations you guys have worked on together, and you make a fine team. Murthy brings the analytical rigor and Sharma has amazing ground level contacts and helps provide inter-departmental collaboration."

"What about Sen, sir?"

This time I kicked Salil under the table for goading Srini, who was clearly going to enjoy what he was going to say, but when he said it, he was dead serious and was looking me in the eye.

"And Sen here, who has real talent for putting enemies in the ground and the moral compass to ensure he does the right thing. In other words, you're a warrior, my boy."

Had Srini just praised me? Stoic Srini, the one who never swore, never laughed too loudly, and had said 'fuck' fewer times than any human being I knew. Praise from him was even better than free buffet breakfast at the Taj.

"I proposed to the PM that we create a new unit with you and your Ops boys."

My eyes lit up. I would get to do something other than sit in office and fill out forms. Srini grinned.

"Unni, Kishore, Pratap and Bahadur all have separately requested to check if they could work for you again, but we'd never have desk jobs for boys like them. Your new unit could use their talents."

"What kind of unit do you have in mind, Sir?"

Srini looked at Sharma.

"This, by the way, is now aligned with your bosses and the PMO. You will all be on this unit, with the Ops boys and we'll provide the admin support you need. You'll probably need to get a new office, but you'll share all the servers and databases that we, the IB and Military Intelligence have. You will all report into me, though Sen will be the operational leader of this unit."

"What will we do, Sir?"

Srini looked at me.

"The kind of work you're good at. The kind of work you've been doing of late. Finding threats and enemies who would sometimes fall between the inter-departmental cracks, which we'd never be able to tackle through official channels and then doing what's needed to neutralize them."

When someone in Srini's position says something like that, in plain English it means that you're being given a license to kill. I was too jaded and too cynical to be excited at solely that thought. I had no delusions of grandeur and knew that I, and men like me, were just tools. Tools which did our jobs well but depending on those who sent us into the field, we could be tools of justice or tools of political expedience. As long as I worked for someone like Srini, I was comfortable with the role I had to play.

"Sen, what do you have in mind? You look thoughtful."

"Sir, I want us to report only to you. No bureaucrats or politicians. You help us manage them. I don't want our boys to be caught up in politics. I hope that's ok."

He nodded.

"Does this unit have a name, Sir?"

Srini looked at Sharma.

"No, but it can be named what you want it to be."

I ventured my suggestion and found everyone nodding.

"Sir, if nobody has any objections, I'd like to call it Unit 22. After the place where I and the Ops boys cut our teeth. We were troublemakers and that is what made us succeed. I suspect for this unit to work, we all need to be willing to be troublemakers. You never officially closed down Unit 22 after we started it as a task force to look into the assassination plot against the US President. If it's okay, I'd like to use that name for this unit."

Srini grinned.

"I have no doubt about your ability to be a troublemaker, Sen."

He whispered to the waiter and to our surprise, he came back with a bottle of wine.

"Let's raise a toast to new beginnings. The new beginning of Unit 22."

***

The next week went in a blur of finding an office. Whatever grandiose notions we had of getting a cool new office were crushed under the reality of no additional admin budgets being available for our unit. So, we settled for an old basement records room in our office. Salil, Sharma and I had a quick brainstorm, and we all liked it for our own reasons. It had a direct exit into the smoking area, where Sharma could light up. I hadn't seen him smoke a lot before, but now he was smoking like a chimney and blaming me for the additional stress which had made him go back to smoking. Salil liked it because the same side exit allowed him to slip away for lunch to our favorite haunt, Tahrir Kabab Corner, without bumping into busybodies from the office, and knowing Salil, to slip off early on Fridays to grab a beer. The boys liked it because we had our own in-house arsenal. I had given them a blank check on what they could get, since I discovered that while our admin budget was limited, the powers that be had decided we could get anything we wanted when it came to killing people or blowing things up. As I looked around, I saw Unni, Pratap, Bahadur and Kishore sitting near the armory, fawning over the new sniper rifles they had got.

I loved the place because once upon a time, I would have laughed at anyone who suggested that I leave the field and go work in an office in Delhi. If they had pushed, I would have said that I would work in an office only if there were no fancy offices, no big bosses looking over your shoulder, just a bunch of us, a team, a unit, getting stuff done together.

This was that place.

When I had been in the field, the enemy was clearer, and the battlefield better defined. Now the enemy could be among us, and the battlefield could be an alley, a hospital, a school. However, some things didn't change. There was a mission to do, not because our bosses wanted it done, but because doing it would prevent harm from coming to others. There were people to protect, not an abstract concept, but real people- our families and others like them, whom our enemies would want to prey on. Yes, there were enough wolves out there, who thought they could prey on those unable to protect themselves. We were the sheepdogs who would stand in their way.

Salil had put up a spray-painted logo, a stylized Unit 22, with his version of our motto below it.

If you see us, you're already dead.

Srini came in, looking at our handiwork and smiling as he called me, Sharma and Salil into our conference room, the only enclosed room in our office.

"Raza has been singing and has given us lots of good stuff. Some of that intel we will act on through regular channels, but I can already see a couple of missions that might be up your alley."

I smiled. It was good to get into the game instead of just waiting.

"We're ready, Sir. How's Raza and more importantly, where is he? Why hasn't the government publicized the fact that we've got him?"

Srini replied with a sheepish smile.

"Politics. Don't be surprised if he's wheeled out just before the elections as a huge triumph for the government. Beyond Raza, there's been some more interesting intel coming our way. From the Brits of all people."

"The Brits?"

"Yes, MI-6 has sent us some credible intel they have of connections between Saudi royalty and terror networks. Most limited to the Middle East, but one of their cells has been active in Kashmir, and we've got some names which we can act upon. That job may go to the Paras but in case it gets politically sticky, it may well come your way."

Sharma asked why it might get politically sticky, but I wasn't listening. My ears had perked up when I heard about Saudi royalty and terror links. Had Aisha given up her secrets to Western Intelligence agencies in return for asylum?

Srini looked at me and coughed gently to get my attention.

"MI-6 is a bit coy about revealing the source of their intel and why they're being so magnanimous in sharing stuff with us, but I asked around. We do have our own contacts in London, and it seems they had a deep cover agent in Saudi who recently escaped."

Srini was looking straight at me, and I could feel my heart pounding so hard I was sure he could hear it. Sharma was staring at me as well, perhaps making the same connections I was.

"It seems the agent was a woman who was there for many years and escaped with her son. Given your recent escapades involving Saudi Royal Guards and runaway princesses, I suppose you know nothing about it, Sen?"

I tried hard to meet his gaze and keep a straight face as I replied.

"Sir, I truly know nothing of any MI-6 agent escaping the Saudis."

"Just as well. The government has had to work really hard to mollify the Saudis after the beating you gave their men and the rumors about one of their princes disappearing while you were there."

***

That evening, I had called Salil and his family over for dinner and we were all sitting in the living room, chatting. When the bell rang, I was surprised to see Rupa Aunty there.

"There you are, young man. Your mother told me you were back. Did you get my lamp?"

I so wanted to tell her that the baboon was lying broken and bloodied in a dustbin somewhere in Dubai after having smashed three goons, but I smiled and apologized for having forgotten it.

She sat down, grabbed a brownie off the plate in front of her and took two big bites, before turning to Ma.

"That's the problem with him. He's always too busy with work. That's why he should get married soon."

Salil looked at me and helpfully suggested that we go get a drink. I thanked him as I went to the kitchen, and we got a beer each.

"I am not going back out there, man. Even chocolate brownies baked by Ma are not worth getting more lectures on matrimonial bliss from Rupa Aunty."

Salil raised his bottle to mine.

"To the joys of remaining single."

His smile disappeared when he saw Bharathi come in behind him.

"Husband dear, you seem to have forgotten the minor detail of us having been married for a dozen years."

Salil was red in the face, and did the only thing he could, which was to drain his bottle as I laughed.

Life was good. I was among family and friends, doing work I enjoyed, with people I liked. But there was something missing. I thought of Aisha, the time we had spent together, and the message she had sent. Yes, it had all meant something, and the only regret I had was that we both lived and worked in a world where two people like us were fated to never be together. But she and Amir were safe, and I hoped the sacrifices she had made in being with someone like Soleiman for so many years had been worth it, that what she had learned was going to be used to keep innocents safe and put the bad guys away.

Salil and Bharathi had gone back to the living room, continuing their banter, and Rupa Aunty came in, brownie in hand, looking for some water. I felt trapped, more trapped that I've ever felt being faced down by a jihadi with an automatic rifle.

"Son, you really should marry. Now, there's nobody else around, so tell your Rupa Aunty what kind of girl do you want to be with?"

I was three beers down, and I had been thinking of Amy and Aisha, so when I blurted out my answer, I could see Rupa Aunty start to choke on her brownie.

"The problem is the girls I like are all assassins or spies. Know any?"

***

AUTHOR'S NOTE

THE REAL-LIFE UNIT 22

While all characters and actions depicted in this novel are fictional, the Special Frontier Force does indeed exist and does indeed report into India's external intelligence agency, the Research & Analysis Wing. It was set up in the aftermath of the 1962 Indo-Chinese war, to conduct covert operations behind Chinese lines. It was initially staffed largely with Tibetan exiles and with officers from elite units in the Indian Army like the Paras. Much of its operational history is shrouded in secrecy to the extent that the SFF is mentioned separately in the 2nd schedule of the Right to Information Act, 2005, which exempts the government from having to furnish any information on it. Over the years, details of some of its exploits have come out into the public domain, including cross-border operations like a daring climb up the 25,645 feet high Nanda Devi mountain in 1965 to install a nuclear-powered transmitter to keep watch on Chinese nuclear and missile activity and the pivotal role it played in operations such as Meghdoot, the capture of the Siachen Glacier in 1986. Today, the SFF is deployed in several operational roles, including counter-terror operations.

Like Major Aaditya Sen and his comrades depicted in the series, the SFF has long enjoyed a fearsome reputation for seizing the initiative and taking the fight to the enemy. Perhaps as a result of cross-border missions which rattled the Chinese, in 1975, the SFF was prohibited from being deployed within 10 kilometers of the Indo-China border unless it was explicitly ordered to do so. Such restrictions, usually placed on fighter planes and strategic assets, being placed on a special forces group, speaks both to the SFF's capabilities and to the strategic and psychological impact it has on adversaries.

The Special Group, which the fictional Major Aaditya Sen served in, is one of the elite elements in the SFF and is often its sword arm for conducting the most hazardous and daring operations. The inspiration for Unit 22 comes from the fact that the SFF is also sometimes known as Establishment 22 or just '22' in honor of its first Inspector General, Maj. Gen. Sujan Singh, who commanded the 22nd Mountain Division in Europe during World War II and later commanded a special forces unit in North Africa. He was a legendary figure in the British Indian Army and won the Military Cross. He and others who followed him created the ethos that has led the SFF to be one of the least known, yet most deadly, of India's special forces, whose men serve in the shadows, to keep us safe.

As Winston Churchill said, "We sleep safely at night because rough men stand ready to visit violence on those who would harm us."

ABOUT MAINAK DHAR

Mainak Dhar wears many hats. He considers his most important job to be the best possible father and husband he can be. An MBA from the Indian Institute of Management, Ahmedabad with over two decades of experience in the corporate world, his 'day job' involves leading businesses and teams as a CEO. A self-described 'cubicle dweller by day and writer by night', when he's not with his family or at work, he loves creating and sharing stories. He is the author of over twenty books, many of which have been bestsellers, including the Alice in Deadland series, 03:02, and Sniper's Eye. His books have been translated into Turkish, Vietnamese, Japanese, French, German, Portuguese and Hindi, with close to half a million copies sold worldwide. He is also a passionate student of Karate and holds a Black Belt. Learn more about him and contact him at www.mainakdhar.com.